CRAZY LOVE

THE SIXTH BUBBA MABRY MYSTERY

Steve Brewer

For Robert & Lauren:
So nice to meet you!
Thanks,
Steve Brewer

INTRIGUE PRESS

Philadelphia

ISBN 1-890768-31-6

First Printing, March 2001

This book is a work of fiction. Names, characters, places and incidents are either the product of the author's imagination or are used fictitiously. Any resemblance to actual events or locales or persons, living or dead, is entirely coincidental. Although the author and publisher have made every effort to ensure the accuracy and completeness of information contained in this book, we assume no responsibility for errors, inaccuracies, omissions, or any inconsistency herein. Any slights of people, places or organizations are unintentional.

Library of Congress Cataloging-in-Publication Data
Brewer, Steve.
    Crazy Love / by Steve Brewer.
        p. cm.
    ISBN 1-890768-31-6 (alk. paper)
    1. Mabry, Bubba (Fictitious character)--Fiction.
    2. Private investigators--New Mexico--Albuquerque--
    Fiction. 3. Albuquerque (N.M.)--Fiction. I. Title.

PS3552.R42135 C73 2001
813'.54--dc21

                                        00-046181

10 9 8 7 6 5 4 3 2 1

"To Kelly, the love of my life."

One

Jealousy sits inside us all, a poisonous little package of possession, wrapped up in our insecurities and bound by need and fear. Unleashed, it's so powerful we'll endanger the love that sparks it, trying to ferret out the truth.

Everything else—love, honor, obedience—lasts only "until death do us part." But jealousy can burn bright as long as one heart beats. And it can make people kill.

Melvin Haywood's jealousy flared after his wife was already in the grave, so I was suspicious when he asked me to find the man who'd made him a cuckold. I had the queasy feeling someone else would end up dead.

I met Haywood at the Olympus Café, a popular joint near the University of New Mexico that has white walls and checked tablecloths and travel posters of Grecian isles on the walls. Crowded as usual, and noisy enough that we didn't have to worry about eavesdroppers. Haywood was a soft-spoken man, and I leaned across the table to hear him over the yakking and clatter. It didn't help that our conversation was interrupted every few seconds by the stout owner, shouting over a loudspeaker that an order was ready. He sounded exasperated, as if he might swat the next customer who didn't respond immediately when a number was called.

"Numbah feefty-two! Feefty-two!"

Every announcement made me check my ticket nervously. It was distracting, but I didn't want to be the laggard who made the harried owner snap.

"Numbah feefty-three! Feefty-three!"

I concentrated on Haywood's face, trying to read his lips.

"Eileen and I were married thirty-three years. We were very happy together. Eileen couldn't have children, so it sometimes felt like something was missing, but we filled the days as best we could. It was a happy marriage."

He kept repeating "happy" like he was trying to reassure himself. He'd said the same thing on the phone when he arranged this lunch meeting two hours earlier. Haywood didn't look happy. He looked, in fact, like a turtle, and turtles aren't known for their expressions of joy. He sat hunched with his balding head thrust forward on a skinny neck. Heavy-lidded eyes blinked slowly behind steel-rimmed eyeglasses, which sat too high on his crooked beak of a nose. He moved slowly, too. Outside, I'd seen him coming a block away, his gray suit out of place here in Birkenstockland, and it had seemed to take ten minutes in the scalding July sun for him to reach me and introduce himself and give me a one-pump handshake. He was around sixty, but I couldn't imagine he'd ever had much spring in his step, which was why I was braced to fetch the food when our number was called.

"Numbah feefty-four! Feefty-four!"

I checked my ticket again. We were next. Sweat trickled down my sides underneath the loose polo shirt. I had my feet under me, my legs cocked to spring up as soon as Number fifty-five was called.

"I never had any reason," Haywood was saying, "to suspect Eileen. She always seemed so loyal, so happy with her lot in life."

"Numbah feefty-four!"

I was halfway out of my chair before I realized it wasn't my turn. I sat down sheepishly, and said to Haywood, "Not us yet. Number fifty-four better hustle it up, or the owner will throw out his food."

Haywood shook his head. "Some people have no patience."

"Guess they're pretty busy here," I said, checking my ticket once more. "You seem like a pretty calm guy yourself."

"In my business, it pays to be patient and careful."

"What business are you—"

"NUMBAH FEEFTY-FOUR!"

I jumped to my feet, then caught myself and lowered onto the edge of my chair.

"Sorry," I said. "I keep thinking that's us and—"

"Numbah feefty-FIVE!"

I leaped up and hurried away to the pickup counter. A fat guy was in front of me, hefting a well-loaded tray, and his face was burning red. Guess he was Number fifty-four. Slowpoke. I traded my ticket for our tray and got the hell away from the counter.

Once I'd set our plates on the table—gyros for Haywood, souvlaki for me—I took a deep breath and some of the tension eased from my shoulders. Maybe now I could tune out the loudspeaker and pay attention to my potential client. Haywood watched me closely, probably wondering why I was so damn jumpy.

The food was worth the jangled nerves. The first bite of skewered pork was crusty on the outside, tender inside, seasoned with a hint of lime. Heaven.

Through a mouthful, I said, "Sorry. You were saying?"

Haywood, chewing methodically, shook his head to show he couldn't remember where the conversation had been interrupted.

"What kind of business are you in?" I asked, proud to be able to pick up the thread.

"Um." He swallowed and his Adam's apple bobbed behind the slack skin of his neck. "I own an accounting firm. MHC Associates. Perhaps you've heard of it?"

I shook my head and stuffed more food in my face.

"I started it right out of college as the Melvin Haywood Company. Just a one-man band in a tiny hole of an office. I married Eileen a few years later and worked hard to make the firm grow. I have a staff of more than thirty now. We handle the accounts of some of the larger companies in town."

Haywood spoke so deliberately, I went through half my souvlaki while he was telling me this. I liked the sound of his profitable firm. Private eyes like it when their clients make plenty of money; a better chance some might come our way.

"And your wife? Did she work?"

Haywood shook his head, took a sip of his iced tea. "Eileen was always content to stay at home. She raised flowers and did charity work and fed the hummingbirds. She was always a very happy person."

"As you said."

"Right. She kept up her pleasant demeanor even after the cancer struck."

"When was that?"

"A year ago next week. We knew it was bad from the initial diagnosis. Pancreatic cancer, and it had already spread to nearby organs. The doctors did all they could, but she died six months later."

Haywood looked so grieved that the food went sour in my mouth.

"I'm sorry."

He shrugged his narrow shoulders deeply. It looked as if he might tuck his head inside there and not come out again.

"Thank you, but I think I'm recovering from the loss. As best as a person can. But the other thing—the item I mentioned on the phone—I can't seem to let it go. It keeps me awake at night, distracted all the time. My business is suffering. I can't seem to get on with my life. I still have trouble believing Eileen would've been unfaithful. She was always so—"

"Happy?"

"Yes, that's it. I never had any indication she might be lonely or unsatisfied."

"Then how do you know she cheated on you?"

Haywood sighed.

"She told me, in a way. Near the end, when it was clear she wasn't going to last much longer. I was sitting by her hospital bed, holding her hand, trying in my awkward way to tell her how much she'd always meant to me. She was in a lot of pain and the drugs didn't seem to be helping. As I said, it was just a matter of time."

This gray little man talking about his wife's death finished off my appetite. I set down my fork and watched pain dance across his face.

"She was still responsive. She answered me one-for-one. I said I always loved her, and she said it back to me. I said I would miss her, and she smiled and said the same. I told her I'd always been faithful to her and a sadness passed across her face."

"And then you knew."

"I didn't want to believe it. I said, 'Eileen?' And I repeated what I'd said about being faithful. I suppose I wanted to make sure she'd heard me right. Give her another chance to say the same to me. But she couldn't. Her eyes filled with tears."

Haywood slowly pushed his plate aside. I guess remembering it all hadn't done much for his appetite either.

"What did you do then?"

Again with the mournful shrug. "What could I do? She was dying. We both knew it. I didn't want to cause her more pain. I changed the subject. I held her hand. I promised myself I wouldn't think about it anymore. For a while, I thought I'd succeeded. But I took her death hard, Mr. Mabry."

"Call me Bubba."

"All right. Bubba."

He screwed up his face when he said it. Some people have a problem with my nickname. Particularly if they've never known any Bubbas or, worse, if they've known several.

"At first, I was too busy grieving to dwell on that conversation with Eileen. It came back to me, though, and it made me hot inside. I couldn't stop thinking about it. I ran a mental inventory of our friends, trying to pick who might've had an affair with her, but I didn't come up with anyone. I thought about the people she saw—at the grocery, at the garden club, at the country club. I'm suspicious of everybody."

Haywood seemed to deflate before my eyes, becoming

smaller in his chair, slumped and ashamed.

"So that's what you want from me? To find out who Eileen had an affair with?"

Haywood sat up straighter and a spark came back to his hooded gray eyes. "That's exactly what I want. I have to know."

"Any idea when she had this affair or how long it might've lasted?"

He shook his head. "I've thought about it for months now, and I don't have a clue."

I cracked my knuckles. If this man, who'd known his wife more than thirty years, couldn't figure it out, how did he expect me to do it?

As if he'd read my mind, Haywood said, "I think people might talk to you. They won't tell me. They try to protect my feelings. They tell me I should forget it and only remember the good things about Eileen. And that's what I want to do. I'll be retiring in a few years. I'd like to think I still have some good years left. But I'll never be able to move on with my life until I know who did it."

Here was a man who never had a reason to be jealous while his wife was alive. A mild little man who knew his place in the world and in his wife's heart. Now his wife was gone and his world had been turned upside down. I thought again of a turtle, stuck on its back, its clawed feet thrashing the air. Melvin Haywood wanted me to set him right again. I could no more turn him down than I could ignore a poor stranded turtle.

Besides, I needed a case. My income had been spotty lately, and I'd caught myself questioning my choice of careers during reruns of *Oprah*. If I could help this man and rake in two hundred a day plus expenses, I couldn't very well turn him down, could I?

But first I had to ask.

"Say I take your case and, against all odds, find this man. What will you do to him?"

Haywood looked at me quizzically. "Do?"

"Most guys in your situation, they'd try to get revenge. I don't want to finger somebody and have him end up hurt or worse. I won't be part of some vengeance trip."

Haywood chuckled and it was the first time he'd looked anything but somber. His mouth widened into a smile, exposing bright dentures, and for a moment I saw what Eileen must've seen in him, more than three decades ago.

"Bubba, do I look like Charles Bronson to you?"

"People do strange things when love and jealousy are involved."

"I'm not after revenge. I just want peace of mind. Can you help me?"

I reached across the table and shook his limp hand.

"I'll do my best."

Two

I wasn't looking forward to digging around in a dead woman's past, but Melvin Haywood's five-hundred-dollar retainer in my pocket eased my dread somewhat.

An hour later, I drove through his plush neighborhood, checking addresses against a list he'd given me of a dozen people, mostly women, who'd known Eileen well. Most lived near Haywood in a walled community called The Manor.

The Manor sits secluded in Albuquerque's North Valley, a verdant area of wineries and mansions and towering cottonwood trees. Two steady infusions keep the valley lush: irrigation water from the nearby Rio Grande and money from the swells who want to maintain the illusion of the bucolic. The fenced pastures were dark green, dotted with black-eyed Susans. Rambling houses rose from the fields at quiet distances from the sweeping curves of Rio Grande Boulevard. Shiny foreign cars nosed up to them like piglets around sows. All the ambient wealth made me more enthusiastic about Haywood's case. He'd given me a nearly impossible task, and the longer it took, the more I'd profit. Any guy who could buy his way into The Manor could afford a long, fruitless investigation.

The Manor was built on land once owned by an eccen-

tric German-born farmer and merchant named Otto
Heilbend. Heilbend bought up hundreds of acres in the
rich valley nearly a century ago. His peons grew apples and
alfalfa and raised horses and goats. In the middle of the
cropland, he built a castle of native stone, complete with
towers and ramparts and a huge Gothic front door.
Heilbend set himself up like a feudal lord and everybody
referred to the place as—you guessed it—The Manor.

Heilbend died broke during the Depression and the castle burned a few years later and it's all ancient history now,
part of Albuquerque's tattered past. But the land still yield-
ed big profits for somebody, sprouting houses, each one
bigger and brassier than the next. The houses sat on half-
acre lots and most had fenced swimming pools out back.
The air reeked of chlorine and flowers and ready cash.

Haywood's house was a pueblo-style adobe big enough
for a whole tribe, with rounded corners and shady patios
and red hummingbird feeders hanging from the trees. I
parked my red Dodge Ram in his driveway, figuring it
might get towed if I left it on the street in this swank neighborhood.

Gardeners and domestics worked around some of the
mansions, but Haywood's place was clearly empty. I imagined him rattling around the house, his footsteps echoing
in the vacuum left by the loss of his wife.

The forlorn image made me glad I had a wife at home,
one who's faithful and in good health. My wife, Felicia
Quattlebaum, is a terrific person, ambitious and strong-
willed and smart. She can be a little irritable at times, a little scary in fact, but I owe her a lot.

I tried to call her on my cellular phone, mostly to crow
about the five-hundred bucks I'd pocketed, but the recep-

tionist at the *Albuquerque Gazette* said she was unavailable. Felicia had been slaving day and night lately on a secret investigative project. I missed her on the nights she worked late, but I tried not to let my resentment show. Felicia's the breadwinner in our household, and if she needs to work all the time, who am I to complain? She's out winning the bread while I'm scrambling for crumbs.

Without Felicia, I'd be poor and lonesome and ill-behaved. I'd been all those things before we met. Living in a cheap motel on East Central Avenue, spending way too much time with criminals and street crazies. These days, thanks to her, I lead a solid middle-class life. We own a brick house near UNM with a spare room I use as my office. Our house is a hovel compared to the palaces in The Manor, but it's a homey little place and we've settled into a domestic routine there. Felicia's long hours had screwed up that routine lately, but then my job tends to have odd hours, too, when I'm lucky enough to have a case.

So I was ambling down a shady sidewalk, thinking happy thoughts about Felicia, when I came to the first address on Haywood's list. Cottonwoods stood sentinel around a lumbering sprawl of white stucco and stained glass. The house rose to a cupola at the front, and I might've mistaken it for a church if it had been located anywhere but The Manor. Flagstones and flowerbeds swept up to the front door in curves designed to slow you down so you had time to admire the place. The door was a beauty of etched glass and oak, wide enough that I could've driven my truck inside. I pushed a button and a bell went bing-bong and I whistled tunelessly while I waited for someone to answer.

I waited a long time. So long, in fact, that I'd given up and was turning away from the door to hunt the next address when I heard the latch click. I wheeled around to find a woman swinging open the big, silent door. The first thing I noticed, naturally, was that she wore a tiny red bikini. The second thing was that she held a tall fruity-looking drink, enough to make a parched private eye's mouth water. Strangely enough, I'd taken in all of the above before I noticed the black pistol in her other hand. She didn't exactly aim it at me, but it was pointed in my general direction and my reaction went something like this: "Holy shit!"

I turned to sprint away, but she said in a lazy drawl, "Relax, honey. I'm not gonna shoot you. Not yet anyway."

Relaxing was out of the question, but I could at least pretend I wasn't frightened. I propped up a quavering smile, and said, "Do you always answer the door like that?"

"What? Wearing my bathing suit?"

"Hell, no. With a gun in your hand."

"This little ol' thing?" She waved it around some more, which made me want to dive into the flowerbeds. "My husband"—she made a face at the word—"makes me carry it whenever someone comes by. I'm all alone here during the day."

She made her eyes go round at this news. I chuckled nervously, and she winked at me and said, "Come on in."

She sashayed back into the cool recesses of the house without waiting to see if I'd follow. I considered a quick tiptoe back to my truck, but I bolstered myself with the thought of Melvin Haywood's money and entered.

"Shut the door behind you, honey," she called from the next room.

That made me uneasy. I shouted back, "Have you put that gun away?"

"Sure. What are you afraid of?"

I swallowed heavily and closed the door. The entryway was shadowy without the daylight spilling in. I peeked around the corner into a huge living room with a beamed ceiling and Mexican rugs on the floor. The sofas were fat and the tables were heavy and the air felt thick. The woman, still wearing only the string bikini, reclined on a low sofa, sipping through a straw, her legs crossed and one bare foot bobbing languidly. The pistol, I was happy to see, sat on the coffee table, looking like a brutal knickknack.

Without the distraction of the gun, I felt free to look her over. She was maybe thirty, very tan, slim and taut, and her blond hair was pulled back in a stubby ponytail. Her face had all the right features in all the right places, including a wide smile she flashed my way.

"Excuse the way I'm dressed," she purred. "I was out at the pool."

"I, um, guessed as much. Are you"—I checked Haywood's list—"Mrs. Andrew Rollins?"

The smile flickered and went out. "My name's Charisse. Are you looking for my husband?"

"No, I wanted to talk to you."

Her smile reignited. It made me nervous.

"Why don't you sit down and tell me who you are and what you want?" She emphasized the last word, loading it with meaning.

I averted my eyes and perched on the end of another low sofa, keeping my distance from Charisse Rollins. I told her my name and who I was working for, then said, "Mr. Haywood tells me you were friends with his late wife, Eileen."

"I knew Eileen," she said. "We all know each other here in The Manor. Most of us hang around here all day while our husbands work. You run into people and get to talking. Eileen was a real nice lady. It made me sad when she got sick. But that's what happens after people reach a certain age. That's one reason I try to enjoy life as much as possible while I'm still young."

She gave me that predatory look again, like I was a slice of life she might enjoy. I cleared my throat and clapped my knees together.

This is an occasional problem for me. Some women have the wrong idea about private eyes. They think we're debonair musclemen, full of derring-do, running around in sports cars, getting into adventures and bedding sleek women. Movies and TV make us out to be romantic figures and some people believe it.

I don't look like a TV star. Far from it. I've got a hangdog face and a flaccid body. I don't like to admit that my brown hair is slowly disappearing, but my forehead keeps getting taller. My idea of snappy clothes is old sneakers and jeans laundered within the past week. I'm lucky to have a woman like Felicia, one who doesn't put much stock in a man's looks.

Despite my decided lack of charm and the fact I drive a noisy truck instead of a Ferrari, I sometimes run into a woman like Charisse Rollins, who makes it clear she'd like to notch a private eye onto her bedpost. I've been tempted at times, but I remain faithful to Felicia. For one thing, I believe in the vows we took ten months ago. A deal's a deal. For another, I'm scared to think what Felicia might do if she caught me stepping out on her.

Of course, maybe Charisse wasn't turned on by the whole private eye thing. Maybe she'd just had too many poolside drinks. Maybe any visitor would've gotten the lip-licking, eye-batting, chest-thrusting flirtation treatment. Maybe deliverymen and exterminators and yard guys all over the city smile in fond remembrance at the mention of her name. None of that mattered. Whatever her game was, I wasn't playing.

"Did Mrs. Haywood ever confide in you?"

"About what?" Charisse still beamed me that molasses smile, but I kept looking down at Haywood's list in my hand, as if my questions were written there. Anything to keep our eyes from meeting suggestively. A man can only stand so much.

"Mr. Haywood believes his wife had an affair during their marriage. It may have been before you even knew her—"

I looked up in time to see her swallow the smile. Her plucked eyebrows crouched over her eyes.

"What the hell are you talking about?"

"Mr. Haywood's wife. An affair?"

"Did Eileen have an affair? Are you shitting me?"

The Southern sweetness had gone out of her voice. I stammered and squirmed, but she was on a roll now.

"I don't know where you're from, buddy. But where I grew up, we had a rule: You don't speak ill of the dead. You ever hear of that?"

"Well—"

"Eileen Haywood was a nice person. I can't believe you're trying to sully her name."

"I'm not! Her husband—"

"Her husband should know better. What kind of a ghoul is he?"

"He seems—"

"Don't say any more. You looked like a nice man, but I

can see I made a mistake. You'd better get out of my house now."

I mumbled an apology, then said, "I'm just doing my job here. Mr. Haywood wants—"

She picked up the gun from the coffee table and casually pointed it my way.

"Maybe I didn't make myself clear," she said.

"I'll just be going."

I didn't run for the door. I have my dignity. But I walked pretty damned fast. All the way to the street.

Three

I wish I could say things improved as the afternoon wore on, but the women of The Manor seemed intent on keeping one another's secrets. Three of them slammed their doors in my face. Another invited me inside, offered me a cold drink, then showed me out again as soon as I asked my initial question. I didn't even get to take a sip.

I was thirsty too. The temperature was in the mid-nineties and the sun beat down on my head like a molten hammer. This time of year, mid-July, we usually have a change in the weather, the arrival of our monsoons. While the rest of the country swelters, New Mexico gets thunderstorms rolling up from the Gulf of California nearly every afternoon. Wind and cloud cover keep the temperature down. Sometimes it even rains. Without the storms, we'd be like Phoenix, where your skin bakes right off your bones.

The monsoons were overdue this year and the whole city seemed to be holding its hot breath, waiting. Maybe that was why all these rich women were so cranky. I searched the clear blue sky while I trudged to the last house I needed to check.

Sweat ran into my eyes as I rang the doorbell. I used the hem of my blue polo shirt to wipe my brow. I was bent over, the tail of my shirt up over my face, my hairy stomach hanging out, when the door opened. I quickly pulled down my shirt and tried a smile. The woman at the door said, "Yes?"

She was a tall, angular woman, around forty years old, with short brown hair and a tanned face and chocolate eyes. She wore khaki pants, canvas sneakers and a crisp white shirt with the sleeves cuffed to her elbows. She was touched by gold here and there—earrings, a chain around her neck, a wedding ring and one thick bracelet. All in all, she was about the most normal-looking person I'd seen all day.

"Hi, my name's Bubba Mabry and I'm a private investigator, doing some work for one of your neighbors. Could I ask you a few questions?"

She glanced up and down the empty street before she said, "Sure, come in."

I followed her into the Mediterranean-style house, which was cool and airy. Like at the Rollins house, the foyer opened into a showplace living room. To my left, tall windows ran down one wall, looking out onto a tailored flower garden. The carpet was thick underfoot and the seating was well-padded leather. Indian pots, each worth more than my annual income, squatted on tables and on the mantel of a fieldstone fireplace.

"Nice place," said I, master of understatement.

"Thank you." She looked me over. "You must be steaming. Would you like a glass of lemonade?"

What I wanted was a cold beer or six, but I was so parched, I would've accepted a glass of whale spit. I said "please" and hung out my tongue to indicate heatstroke. She strolled across the huge room and through a door on the far side. I settled onto a leather sofa and my sweaty shirt stuck to it. I feared I'd leave a puddle of perspiration behind, but it sure felt good to be off my feet. She returned with a tall glass and smiled as she handed it over. I guzzled down half of it and felt a little better.

"My name's Nancy Chilton," she said, "but you probably already knew that."

"Yes, ma'am. Your name was on a list given to me by Melvin Haywood."

Her brow knitted. "Poor Melvin. I haven't seen much of him lately. How's he holding up?"

"I met him for the first time today. He seems to still be mourning his wife."

"They had a special relationship. They've lived here in The Manor for years. Good people."

The preliminaries were out of the way and I didn't have any choice but to bring up the ugly questions. I took another swallow of lemonade first, figuring I wouldn't be sitting here long once she heard what I wanted.

"Mr. Haywood's given me a strange assignment," I said, willing to pin the blame on Melvin. "Before she passed away, Mrs. Haywood hinted that she'd had an affair sometime during their marriage."

Nancy Chilton's eyebrows arched at this news, but she didn't herd me toward the door. Not yet, anyway.

"He's done the forgiving part," I said quickly, "but he can't seem to forget. He says he can't sleep at night, too worried about who might've been involved in this infidelity."

She shifted in her chair and the leather cushion sighed.

"I know this seems untoward," I said. "But Mr. Haywood feels he can't rest until he knows who it was. Any way you could help me?"

Nancy Chilton glanced around the room, as if searching for an exit, but finally she took a deep breath and answered.

"I may know something about this, but I'm not sure I should talk about it. Eileen told me about it in secret. It's a private matter."

"Yes, ma'am. I understand your concern." I talked faster. I felt like I had a fish on the line and I didn't want to let her get away. "It'll be kept strictly confidential. It's just to ease Mr. Haywood's mind."

She got up and wandered about the room, touching the furniture and straightening the etched black pots on the mantel. I held my breath.

"What's Melvin going to do to this person when he finds out?" she asked finally.

I gulped air and said, "I asked the same question. I was worried he might try to get revenge on the guy. But he promises that's not the case."

She smiled. "No, I can't imagine Melvin Haywood harming anybody. He's such a mild little man."

I opened my mouth to ask whether she agreed that he resembled a turtle, then thought better of it. She returned to her chair and perched on the edge of the seat.

"All right," she said, and her eyes sparkled. "I'll tell you what I know, but I don't want to be connected to it in any way. Don't tell Melvin who told you."

I nodded. After my sweltering, unproductive afternoon, I would've agreed to most anything to make some progress.

She leaned forward and lifted the lid of a large, ornate box on the heavy coffee table. She pulled out a brown cigarette and used a lighter to flick it to life. She took a deep drag and watched me as she blew out a cloud of smoke.

"This bother you?" she asked.

"Not at all. Smells good. I used to be a smoker myself."

"Overcame it, huh?"

"Hardest thing I ever did." I didn't mention that the impetus for quitting had been that I was flat-ass broke at the time.

She gave me a wry grin and said, "I don't smoke much anymore, but I can't help myself when it's time to gossip."

Lord love a busybody! Nancy Chilton was just what I needed.

She took another drag on the cigarette and looked around for an ashtray. Finding none handy, she tapped the ashes into the cupped palm of her left hand.

"You have to understand something," she said. "Here in The Manor, people have too much money and too little to do. We fill our days as best we can—I play a lot of tennis—but idleness leads to people messing around and that leads to gossip. You follow me?"

Like Mary's little lamb. I nodded briskly.

"I know gossip is terrible, but I can't help myself," she said. "We're all stuck here, walled off from the world. I can't tell you how many hours I sat around with Eileen Haywood, drinking coffee and dishing."

I cleared my throat, guessing that Nancy Chilton did most of the talking at those sessions. "It was during one of these conversations that she told you her secret?"

Nancy nodded. She seemed in no hurry, as if she wanted to savor the secret before spitting it out.

"We'd been talking for hours," she said. "It was during spring planting season and we were sitting out in the garden with dirt under our fingernails and sweat in our hair."

"And talking," I urged.

She inhaled more smoke and dumped more ashes into her palm. God, the anticipation! I wanted to rush her along, make her get to the point, but I could see it wouldn't do any good. She was enjoying herself too much to be hurried.

"I told Eileen I was worried about my husband, Boyd. He's that car dealer here in town, does those TV commercials, wears a big cowboy hat?"

I nodded some more. If she was married to that blowhard, no wonder she looked for ways to amuse herself.

"I was worried Boyd might be having an affair. Eileen talked me down out of my tree, told me Boyd's not the type who'd play around. Which is a load of horse manure, but it helped at the time. Then she confessed she'd once fooled around behind Melvin's back. Why, you could've knocked me over with a feather! Sweet little Eileen Haywood? I never would've believed it if anyone else had told me."

"Did she give you the particulars?"

"Some. I could tell it made her uncomfortable, so I changed the subject after a while. And I never brought it up again. It was our secret."

"Did she say who the man was?"

Nancy Chilton nodded and smoked some more and tapped more ashes into the growing pile in her cupped hand. The brown cigarette was almost gone, which meant she'd be getting up and searching down an ashtray soon. Another interruption. I thought I'd scream if she didn't give me a name soon.

"He's a doctor, lives right here in The Manor. I was surprised, that's for sure."

She looked around again for an ashtray. I jumped up and offered her my lemonade glass, which was now empty except for a couple of ice cubes. She made a face, but she went ahead and dumped the ashes into the glass. The butt sizzled against the ice. Nancy Chilton brushed off her hands and sat back, enjoying my impatience.

"He's a sports doctor. Made a fortune specializing in busted knees and torn ligaments and stuff like that. Half the people in The Manor have used him. I even go to him myself to get treated for tennis elbow."

"And this doctor, does he have a name?"

She grinned. "Andrew Rollins. Ever heard of him?"

I guess my face showed shock because she chuckled. I stammered for a second before I said, "Charisse's husband?"

"You know Charisse?"

"No, not at all." The denial sounded a little embarrassed in my own ears. "I mean, I met her today. Her house was the first place I stopped to ask questions."

"Is that right?" Nancy Chilton made no effort to hide her distaste. "And what did young Charisse tell you?"

"She ran me out of her house at gunpoint."

Nancy laughed uproariously. When she could get a grip on herself, she said, "That sounds like Charisse, always waving that pistol around. It's a wonder she didn't try to sleep with you first, though. That's the usual pattern."

I started to say I'd suspected as much, but caught myself and clammed up. The residents of The Manor might engage in such gossip, but I didn't need to join them. Besides, I wasn't sure I hadn't misread that whole come-on from Charisse. And heaven help me if it ever got back to Felicia.

"This thing with Eileen was before the good doctor married Charisse," Nancy said. "Charisse is his third wife. Every one a bimbo, if you ask me. Little trophies he keeps around to make him feel young. When they start to show their years, he trades them in for a new model."

"A common syndrome," I said.

"Dr. Andrew makes an art of it. And I think he still sleeps

with his patients whenever he feels like it. What's Charisse going to do? Divorce him? If it weren't for his money, she wouldn't have a pot to pee in."

Nancy leaned forward, her elbows on her knees. She was talking excitedly now, letting it all spew out.

"Anyhow, this thing with Eileen came three or four years ago when Andrew was in the midst of divorcing Wife Number Two. Eileen said she broke it off after only a few trysts. She felt terribly guilty and she worried Melvin might find out. She made me promise not to tell anyone, and I kept that promise until just now."

I doubted that. Nancy Chilton clearly loved to gab. She was about the last person I would've trusted with a secret. But I didn't say so.

"Andrew met Charisse on a plane not long after that. She was a stewardess." Nancy pretended to gag herself. "I guess Charisse knows an opportunity when she sees one because they soon were married. If you ask me, Andrew finally got what he deserved. She runs around on him, spends his money. They're a perfect match, really."

I stood and wiped my hands on my shirt. They felt sticky and soiled and I didn't think it was just from the heat outside. Nancy Chilton was telling me more than I wanted to know about the residents of The Manor. I had the name I needed. Time to escape.

She looked ready to say more, but I said, "I won't take up any more of your time. Thanks so much for your help."

Nancy Chilton smiled stiffly and rose to follow me to the door.

If she was right, I was close to solving Melvin Haywood's case. So much for that gravy train I thought I'd ride a while. I'd have to check it out, naturally. Gossips like

Nancy Chilton are notoriously unreliable. But that wouldn't take long. Shit. I needed to stretch it out another day or two just to keep the retainer.

When we reached the door, I thanked her again. Her smile had evaporated and she looked worried.

"You're not going to tell Melvin I told you about this, right?"

"He's only interested in the name, not in how I got it."

"Promise?"

I nodded, hoping it was the truth.

Then she surprised me, asking for my business card. I fished one out of my wallet and handed it over.

"In case you think of something else?" I ventured.

"I"ve told you all I know about poor Eileen. But who knows? I might need a private investigator sometime."

I wondered about that all the way back to my truck.

Four

I keep a phone book under the seat in my truck, along with flashlights and old rags and camera gear and other crap essential to a private investigator. Now that my wife has forced me to carry a cellular phone everywhere I go, I find that having phone numbers handy saves on those rip-off Directory Assistance charges. More importantly, a phone book is full of addresses.

Most private eye work, which seems so glamorous in movies, is just a matter of knocking on enough doors. Years ago, I worked with an investigator, Bill Pomfrey, who kept in his car a "criss-cross," one of those reverse directories that lists everybody by address. Bill could go up to any door in town and greet the occupant by name. He claimed it made a world of difference in his interviews. I've never tried it. Those directories cost something like six hundred bucks and they have to be updated every year. To hell with that. I figure, "What's your name?" is as good an opening as any.

But your standard phone book worked plenty well when it came to finding Dr. Andrew Rollins. Charisse had told me he was at work and Nancy had told me about his fancy sports medicine clinic. The phone book told me the clinic was on Lomas Boulevard just west of downtown, in an area where lots of old bungalows have been remodeled into law offices and the like. I was there in ten minutes.

Rollins' building was a modern brick job the color of ripe apricots. The one-story building was set back from the busy four-lane street to leave room for a parking lot that wrapped around it on two sides. The clinic apparently was doing a land-sale business; all the parking slots were full. I left the Ram on the street and walked toward the clinic entrance, wondering how to broach Rollins' long-ago dalliance with Eileen Haywood.

Normally, I avoid doctors' offices at all costs. Too many germs floating around in the waiting rooms. You usually emerge sicker than when you entered. But I figured I was safe this time. Sports doctors deal with injuries, not illnesses, and it's pretty hard to catch tennis elbow or ruptured tendons from somebody else.

The waiting area was carpeted and comfortable and quiet. Crutches leaned next to long-suffering patients who occupied the plump furniture, leafing through magazines. The far end of the waiting room had a counter with a window where you could check in for your appointment. I walked up to it and peered inside. The usual desks and file cabinets filled the small room beyond, but no people were visible. On the counter sat a clipboard with a sign-in sheet for patients. A lot of names remained to be crossed out. Next to the clipboard was a bell like you find in hotels and I gave it a slap. The bell sounded loudly in the quiet office, and I winced and glanced over my shoulder. Several patients glared at me. I wrote my name and time of arrival on the sign-in sheet while I waited. After a minute or so, a wide-bodied nurse rumbled into the reception office.

She had a face like a bulldog and a build like a 747. Her underslung jaw was draped on either side by sagging

cheeks, giving her a perpetual frown. Beady black eyes sized
me up and found me wanting. She wore white head-to-toe
and an old-fashioned nurse's hat on top of whetstone-gray
hair cut brutally short. The hat made me think of nuns, the
type that crack student knuckles with their rulers.

"Yes?" She made the word a question, but just barely.
Her tone was very nearly a challenge, one that said, "You're
already wasting my time. Tell me what you want."

"Hi, uh—" I looked at the nametag pinned to her
expansive breast. "Hildegarde Wyborn, R.N." Better not try
using her name. And definitely push aside those wiseass
thoughts about calling her "Sister Hildegarde."

"My name's Bubba Mabry," I said. "Here's my card."

I slid one of my flimsy cards across the counter so she
could read it. She glanced down at the card, but didn't touch
it. Her stout hands were clasped before her waist, the thumbs
tapping together with impatience. If she was surprised that a
private eye had come calling, she didn't show it.

"I need to speak to Dr. Rollins," I said, keeping my voice
low rather than risking an uprising among the impatient
patients.

She nodded curtly toward the waiting room. "Dr. Rollins
is very busy today. Perhaps you'd like to leave a message."

No, that wouldn't do. I needed to talk to Rollins face to
face, see his reaction when I mentioned Eileen Haywood.

"It will only take a minute," I said. "I just need to ask
him a few questions."

"About what?"

"Afraid that's private."

She glowered at me. "Then I'm afraid you're out of luck.
Dr. Rollins sees no one without an appointment."

"But I'm not sick," I protested, which caused some

grumbling in the waiting room. "I mean, I don't need to see him as a patient. I have questions about another matter."

She was shaking her head before I finished. It made her jowls slop about, and I leaned back automatically, as if she truly were a bulldog who might sling drool on me. She scowled harder.

"Dr. Rollins is completely booked up today. If you want to leave your card, or if you want to call tomorrow—"

"No, no, no. It has to be today. Right now."

Why was I so insistent? Another day would mean I could keep Haywood's retainer with a clear conscience. But I felt compelled to force the issue, Hildegarde Wyborn be damned.

Looking back, I understand my motive. I was within inches of solving a case in a single afternoon. That had never happened before. The business hadn't been going so well lately; maybe I was trying to prove something. At the time, I had none of these thoughts. I just wanted to see Rollins and this chunky nurse seemed to be all that stood in my way.

"Look," I said, trying a bluff, "I don't want to bring the police into this."

Her BB eyes shot past me to the waiting patients. "Keep your voice down. No need to make a scene."

"I don't want a scene. I don't want any trouble. But if you don't fix it so I see Rollins, and I mean right now, we're all going to be on the six o'clock news."

Bold, eh? Pure bluff. Spoken with the confidence of a man holding a royal flush when in fact I was looking at deuces and treys. If she said no, I had no recourse. I'd just cash in my chips and go home. But she didn't know that. She studied me carefully for a moment, her thick thumbs still tapping together. Then she nodded brusquely and waddled away. I waited, peering through the window, wondering whether I would've been so bold if there hadn't been a counter separating me from the beefy nurse.

Then a door opened behind me and Nurse Wyborn said in a frosty voice, "If you'll just step this way."

I turned to follow her through the door, ignoring the shifting and muttering among the waiting patients. Screw 'em, I thought, they should learn to be more assertive. Like me.

I followed the nurse down a hall lined with doors. Most were closed, but one opened into a gymnasium with pads on the walls and barbells and medicine balls sitting around, doing nothing. A redhead in a snug green leotard occupied a weight machine against the far wall, doing some exercise that required her to open her legs wide. She was red-faced and sweaty and she scowled at me when she caught me watching. I hurried along, catching up to Nurse Wyborn just as she reached the door to Rollins' private office. I knew we'd arrived at our destination because the door had the doctor's name on it, along with the word "Private." They don't call me a "detective" for nothing.

The nurse gestured me inside. I sidled through the doorway to keep from brushing against her white prow.

"Take a seat," she said. "Someone will be right with you."

I thanked her and sat in an armchair. She shut the door and went away. Only then did what she'd said sink in completely. "Someone" would be right with me? I didn't want to talk to "someone." I wanted to see Rollins.

I sat there, filled with indecision, wondering whether I should run out the door and chase down Nurse Wyborn and start all over again. But, hell, I'd gotten this far, completely on deception and demand, maybe I shouldn't push my luck. I settled back in the cushy chair to see what would come next.

I didn't have to wait long. The door swung open with enough force to send it thudding into the wall. The doorway was filled jamb to jamb by a huge man. I think I gulped.

He crossed meaty arms over his chest and stared down at me. He was so tall, he only cleared the top of the doorway by an inch or so. I glanced at his feet to see if he was on stilts. No dice. Just your basic white sneakers, which matched the trousers and the T-shirt that were stretched tight over his well-defined body. He looked to be about my age—thirty-seven—and he probably weighed close to three hundred pounds, but if there was any fat on him, it was well-hidden. He had a thick mustache and black hair and a heavy brow that made me think of Goliath in the Bible. And there I sat, without my slingshot.

I leaped to my feet, but I still had to lean backward to look him in the eye. He didn't look happy. Nowhere to run in the tidy office and no squeezing past him through the door. Time to start talking.

"Hi, my name's Bubba Ma—"

"I know who you are," he rumbled. He opened one of his umbrella-sized hands to show my crumpled card in his palm. "The question is: What the hell do you want?"

I swallowed heavily and opened my mouth. Nothing came out. I wanted to chatter away, to bluff this enormous man the way I had the nurse. But fear will steal your voice.

Finally, I managed, "Dr. Rollins?" My voice came out taut and squeaky. I sounded like new sneakers on a hardwood floor.

"You think I'm Rollins?"

I started to shake my head, but my neck felt stiff. Maybe
it was because I had it bent backward, looking up at him.
Then something happened that took some of the tension
away. The giant smiled, exposing big white teeth that were
too perfect to be natural. He even chuckled a little, which I
took as a good sign.

"You've got the wrong guy. My name's Salisbury, Ed
Salisbury. I work for Rollins."

My mind whirred, wondering why Rollins would need
a bouncer at his clinic. Before I could conclude that it was
to keep people like me away, Salisbury explained.

"I'm the Number Two guy around here, in charge of
physical therapy and the exercise programs. Rollins is busy,
seeing patients. Nurse Wyborn told me she informed you
of that, but you were a pushy little bastard who wouldn't
take 'no' for an answer."

The smile vanished as Salisbury remembered I was wasting his time. "Which brings us back to the original question. What the hell do you want?"

I cleared my throat and hacked and stuttered, but finally
got it out.

"I've been hired by one of Dr. Rollins' neighbors. I need
to interview him about something that happened a long
time ago."

Salisbury's stare didn't waver. "And what would that be?"

"Well, it's a confidential matter, if you know what I
mean. I'm sure Dr. Rollins wouldn't want me to—"

Salisbury rolled his shoulders and I swear I could feel a
breeze from the motion. His big jaw jutted out from under
his woolly mustache.

"Look, peanut, I'm gonna say this once. Maybe you
could dance around a nurse and get this far, but I'm not

buying it. She said you made some remark about getting
the police involved. Involved in what?"

I tried smiling at him, but it didn't take. "I may have
overstated the case a little there—"

Salisbury sucked one of his perfect front teeth, which
made his face shift around. Even his cheeks had overdevel-
oped muscles. He looked like he could bite through a
phone book.

"No cops?"

"No cops. I'm just sort of desperate to speak to Dr.
Rollins and I thought if I mentioned the police—"

"So you're a liar."

I shrugged. I could've protested, could've explained that
creative falsehoods are part of my job, but "liar" seemed to
sum it up pretty well.

"Look, I'm sorry if I've caused a problem. If you could
just tell Dr. Rollins I'm here, maybe he'd spare me a minute.
Then I'll get out of here and you'll never see me again."

Salisbury snarled, but a disembodied voice said, "Ed?" I
looked all around the office, but we were still alone. I did-
n't see an intercom or a speaker or any other device that
might've produced the sound.

Then Salisbury turned and I got a glimpse of a man hidden behind him in the hall. He was a slight, short man in a
white lab coat. He had a stethoscope around his neck and a
clipboard in one hand. Like me, he was leaning back to
look up at Salisbury.

"What's going on in there?"

Before Salisbury could answer, I said, "Dr. Rollins?"

He nodded, peering past Salisbury's bulging chest at me.
If Hildegarde Wyborn was a bulldog, Andrew Rollins was a
spaniel. Large, dark, watery eyes with bags under them. A

long, straight nose tilted up on the end. Thinning hair dyed jet-black, which emphasized the lines on his face and his indoor pallor. I guessed he was about fifty. He kept his pointy chin lifted high, which gave him an air of superiority. All in all, just the sort of prosperous little dude I'd love to push around, if only he didn't have Colossal Man on his payroll.

"I'm a private investigator, working for your neighbor, Melvin Haywood. I need to ask you a few questions, but your assistant here—"

"Questions about what?" Rollins asked sharply.

"If I could just have a moment in private?"

Rollins glanced up the hallway, as if he could hear his patients calling. Then he shrugged and said, "Very well."

Salisbury stepped toward me to clear the doorway. Rollins slipped into the office past him and walked around the desk to sit behind it. I returned to my chair. Salisbury closed the door and leaned against it. His presence seemed to fill the small office and the air felt thin, like he was using it all up to fuel the huge engine that was his body.

I risked a glance at him over my shoulder, then looked back at Rollins.

"Don't worry," the doctor said. "Anything you need to tell me, Ed can hear. He's my right-hand man."

"Okay. It's kind of a delicate matter."

"Just ask your questions," Rollins snapped. "I've got patients waiting."

"Right. Um, see, Mr. Haywood hired me to investigate his late wife."

"Eileen?"

"Right."

"What's to investigate? She's dead."

"Right again. But something she said on her deathbed has been bugging Mr. Haywood and he asked me to check it out."

I explained about the infidelity and Haywood's sleepless reaction to it. I watched Rollins closely while I told the story, but there was no shift in his expression, no sign he might be the guilty party. If anything, he looked more impatient than before.

"What does all this have to do with me?" he demanded. "I barely knew Eileen."

I shifted in my chair. I was nervous about asking the pertinent question. Having Salisbury breathing down my neck didn't help.

"One of your neighbors said, uh, that maybe, you know, you were the one."

"One what?"

"The one who had an affair with Eileen Haywood."

Salisbury snorted behind me, but I didn't turn around. Rollins glanced up at his assistant and then back at me.

"Who said that?"

"I'm sorry, I really can't say—"

"One of my neighbors? Goddamn, what a bunch of malicious gossips."

Rollins frowned, staring down at his desk blotter, probably running an inventory of neighbors. I guessed it wouldn't take him long to come up with Nancy Chilton. When he looked at me, his eyes had narrowed and he had a red spot on each cheek.

"I hate this," he said. "People spread gossip and bird dogs like you lap it up."

I hesitated. Rollins seemed angry enough to do something drastic, like maybe turning Salisbury loose on me.

That would be a short and bitter end.

I worked up my courage and said, "So it's not true?"

"I'm not going to dignify that with an answer," Rollins said. "A fucking private eye. That's what I need, somebody poking around in my life. I hate snoopers like you, digging around in the dirt, trying to uncover people's secrets."

I opened my mouth to object to this characterization, even if it was close to the truth, but I didn't get a chance to say anything. One of Salisbury's huge hands clamped down on my shoulder. It felt like it weighed thirty pounds.

"How about it, doc? Want me to show this guy the door?"

Rollins took a deep breath, like he was trying to relax, and I felt sure he would tell his assistant to unhand me. But he said, "Please."

Salisbury palmed my shoulder like it was a basketball and yanked me to my feet.

"Hey now—"

His other hand clamped onto the back of my neck and I forgot what I was going to say. Salisbury turned me toward the door like I was a windup toy. He let go of my shoulder long enough to fling open the door. He went to march me through it, but Rollins' voice stopped him.

"Ed?"

This is it, I thought. Rollins has come to his senses. He'll tell Salisbury not to rough me up.

"Yeah, doc?"

"Don't be too gentle about it."

I swiveled my head to glance up at Salisbury. He was smiling.

"You got it."

He steered me out the door and down the hall. I tried to

protest, but he squeezed the back of my neck tighter and I clammed up. Better to be silent, and still conscious.

He shoved me through the door into the waiting room, and the sight of all those patients gave me hope. Surely, Salisbury wouldn't pound me right in front of his clientele. A couple of jocks seated near the door grinned as he pushed me past them.

The front door was glass and we approached it pretty quickly and I thought for a moment Salisbury planned to use my head as a battering ram. But he reached out and pushed it open and thrust me out into the afternoon heat. He still had my neck in his viselike grip and I felt his other hand grasp my belt and I had time to think something along the lines of "Oh, shit" before he lifted me off the ground and tossed me out into the parking lot. I sailed through the air like Superman, and the first thing to hit the hot asphalt was my belly. All the air whooshed out of me as I skittered across the pavement and rolled onto my side and curled into an aching ball.

Salisbury brushed his hands together as if cleaning them and turned to go back inside. The door whispered shut behind him, but not before I heard him say, "Sorry about the disturbance, folks. I had to take out the trash."

If I'd hoped for outrage from the patients, I didn't get it. Instead, I heard laughter.

I lay there awhile, assessing the damage, wondering if all my bones were intact, but finally there was nothing to do but get up and dust myself off and limp back to my truck, my tail between my legs.

Damn.

Five

I was sure to be a kaleidoscope of bruises later, but the only place requiring immediate attention was my left elbow. I'd scraped it as I was bouncing off the asphalt, leaving a round wound the size of an Oreo. It didn't bleed profusely. Just a steady seep that required me to hold an unsanitary rag on it while I drove.

Felicia wasn't home when I got there, which was too bad. I could've used someone to help me limp into the house. Plus, a dose of sympathy would've been sweet. Not that there was any guarantee Felicia would be sympathetic. When my chosen profession results in physical harm, she usually lectures me on how I ought to have a Real Job.

I got out of the Ram and gimped up the front stoop and let myself into the cool house. Peeling off my sweaty polo shirt was an adventure in pain, but I managed as I shuffled into the bathroom.

I washed my hands and face in the sink and studied my reflection in the mirror, looking for unsightly bulges that might indicate broken ribs. The soft flesh on my abdomen was raw and red from my belly flop on the pavement, but I didn't see anything to indicate I was permanently damaged. At least I hadn't landed on my face. My features aren't anything to brag about, but I like their current arrangement just fine.

I took some aspirin, then got out the peroxide and some gauze and tape to bandage my seeping elbow. It's a comment on the hazards of my occupation and my general clumsiness that Felicia keeps first-aid supplies fully stocked.

I don't know if you've ever tried to tape a bandage on your own elbow, but it ain't easy. For one thing, you can only use one hand while the other dangles uselessly at the end of the injured arm. For another, you can't really see all the way around to your elbow's backside, even with a mirror. I spun around, trying to find the best combination of view and access, and finally got a bandage more or less in place. It wouldn't allow me to bend my elbow much, but I figured it didn't matter. That joint would be so stiff by morning, I wouldn't be able to bend it anyway.

I found a fresh shirt—one that buttoned so I didn't have to pull it over my head—and put it on as I limped into the kitchen for a Heineken.

It was nearly five o'clock and I remembered that I should call Melvin Haywood before he left the office for the day. I guzzled some beer first.

A receptionist put me right through to Haywood's extension.

"Hello, Bubba. What news?"

I stifled a burp and told him I had some progress to report.

"Really? That was quick."

"Well, it's nothing certain yet. I've got more digging around to do."

"But you have a lead?"

A lead? Apparently, Haywood watched detective shows on TV, too. Everybody knows the jargon.

"Yeah. One of your neighbors told me Eileen confided

in her about the affair."

A long pause while Haywood absorbed this. I drank more beer.

"Who's the neighbor?"

"She asked me not to reveal her name."

Another pause.

"Let me ask you something, Bubba. Who's paying your fee again?"

"Look, Mr. Haywood, I don't want to upset you, but I told her I'd keep her name out of it. Doesn't matter anyway. All she had was a tip. I've still got to get some proof."

Haywood exhaled loudly into the phone. It sounded like he was bracing himself.

"Okay, Bubba. Tell me who did it. Who had an affair with Eileen?"

"You sure you're ready to hear this? Maybe we ought to talk in person."

"No, go ahead. I've been thinking about this for months. I can't wait any longer."

"Okay, but like I said, I don't have any proof. I thought I should see if you could shed any light on how well Eileen knew this man, whether there was ever any indication—"

"Just tell me."

Now it was my turn to take a deep breath. "Your neighbor. Andrew Rollins."

This revelation was greeted by such a long silence that I finally said, "Mr. Haywood?"

"I'm here. I'm stunned, that's all. Right there in my own back yard."

"Remember, it might not be true. I talked to Rollins and he didn't act guilty."

"Did he deny it?"

"Not exactly. He said he wouldn't dignify my questions with answers. He was pretty pissed off that I'd asked at all."

"That would seem to indicate guilt to me."

"It was more like he thought the question was some kind of affront. Which I guess it was, in a way. Anyway, he had his big assistant throw me out of his office."

"Throw you out? You mean, physically?"

"Oh, yeah."

"Are you hurt?"

"I've had worse."

"I can't believe Rollins would do something like that. He must've been really angry."

"He was. And not just about my questions. He was pissed because I interrupted his workday. He had a lot of patients waiting."

"Yes, he has a very successful practice," Haywood said, his voice changing so he sounded like the accountant he was. "Everyone from pro athletes to the ladies of The Manor. Eileen even went to see him once for problems with an arthritic knee."

"Is that right? When was that? Maybe that's when the affair began."

"I don't remember when it was, Bubba. But, my God, he hardly needed her to come to the clinic. We've lived near each other for years."

"Right, right. Still, it wouldn't hurt to know. I've got an idea about when the affair occurred. My informant said it happened while he was between wives."

Silence. I worried Haywood was letting his anger take over.

"Remember, Mr. Haywood, you promised you wouldn't do anything to the guy."

"I remember," he said flatly. He sounded as if he regret-
ted making the deal with me.

"And remember this, too: We don't know for sure that
Rollins was the one. My source may be full of it. That happens sometimes."

Haywood pondered that for a moment, then said, "No,
I'm sure your informant has it right. Rollins has always
been something of a hound. Even with a young wife waiting at home, he's always on the prowl."

I didn't ask how Melvin Haywood might know that. I
guessed he wasn't impervious to the neighborhood gossip.
Funny, though, how the gossips rarely tell the affected parties. If Nancy Chilton knew about an affair between Eileen
and Andrew Rollins, then it was a sure bet that others in The
Manor knew, too. Despite what she'd said about protecting
Eileen's secret, I couldn't see Nancy keeping her mouth shut
when she had such a juicy morsel. But nobody told poor
Melvin his wife had stepped out on him. He had to find it
out when it was too late to make it right.

"I'm going to do some more poking around tomor-
row," I told him. "See if I can confirm this tip. If Rollins and
Eileen really did have an affair, somebody's got to know
about it. Somebody saw them or heard something.
Somebody has some proof."

Haywood hesitated before he said, "Yes, I suppose that
would be best. But I'd believe it was Andrew Rollins. The
man has always been a scoundrel."

Scoundrel? If that was the worst Haywood could come
up with, maybe there was no reason to fear he'd seek
revenge. I call people worse names when they cut me off in
traffic.

"He certainly acted like one with me today," I said.

Haywood said nothing, and I could picture him lost in thought, blinking at a changed world with his turtle eyes.

"Okay, Bubba," he said finally. "Thanks for the update. I'll expect to hear from you tomorrow."

"You all right, Mr. Haywood? Do you need to talk about it some more or anything?"

"I'll be fine. I need some time to adjust to the idea that Rollins screwed me this way."

Me thinking: It wasn't you he was screwing, Melvin. But all I said was good-bye. I hung up the phone with my good arm and hobbled off to the fridge for another beer.

Six

By the time Felicia got home, I'd performed the Heineken Maneuver enough times that I was no longer choking with indignation over my treatment at Rollins' clinic. I'd spent a couple of hours lying on the sofa, slugging beers and flipping through TV channels, and had gone stiff as a deacon from my injuries. I could barely sit up when Felicia came puffing through the door, her hair mussed and her cheeks glowing.

"What's the matter with you?" A fine greeting, but typical of Felicia. She's so sharp, nothing gets by her. Of course, the bloodied white bandage on my elbow was a telling clue, along with my robot-like movements as I struggled to get up off the couch.

"A giant threw me across a parking lot. It's a long story."

She stopped where she was and squinted at me through her square eyeglasses.

"You working, or just tangling with a giant for the fun of it?"

I picked up Melvin Haywood's five-hundred-dollar check from the coffee table and waved it at her. I'd left it there so I could look at it occasionally and remind myself there was a sound financial reason for hurting this bad.

"Good case?" she asked as she took the check from

me and looked it over.

"Not so far. I'll tell you about it over dinner."

"You haven't eaten already? It's late."

"I was waiting on you."

Felicia shook her head. "You should've gone ahead. I don't have time to eat. I just came by to change into some jeans and then I'm headed back to the office."

"You've got to work some more?" I moaned.

"Hot story," she said, as if that explained everything.

Her heels clacked on the hardwood floor as she blew through the living room toward our bedroom closet. Limping along behind her, I noticed she was wearing a blue blazer with matching skirt. Hose and heels. Not like Felicia at all. She'd left before I was out of bed that morning, and I hadn't known.

"You're all dressed up."

"Spent the day meeting with attorneys."

"Yuck."

"I thought I ought to dress the part, at least this once. We're trying to persuade our attorneys to let us run this project, which is sure to generate lawsuits."

"How did it go?"

She shrugged off her blazer and threw it haphazardly onto a hanger.

"Okay, I guess. I'll know more tomorrow. You know how these attorneys are."

"Chickenshit."

"Exactly."

"What's got them scared this time?"

She peeled off her blouse. She was wearing a lacy black bra and the sight of it made me forget my pains for a second. If my expression showed any hint of lust, Felicia didn't notice. She was too busy stepping out of her skirt.

"This project's going to make a bunch of car dealers look very bad. Probably result in criminal charges. The dealers won't take it lying down."

Lying down sounded like a very good idea about now, particularly if I could get Felicia to lie down with me. She'd worked so many long hours lately, our sex life was on its deathbed. A little cuddling, a light massage, might do something to help my stiff muscles. I reached out and stroked her shoulder, hooked a finger under her bra strap. She twisted away and frowned at me.

"Come on, Bubba. I'm late already. Jake is waiting for me at the office."

Jake. I'd certainly heard plenty about Jake Steele lately. He was a refugee from TV news who'd signed on with the *Albuquerque Gazette* when he moved back to his hometown from a bigger market back East. He'd only been at the newspaper a few months, but the editors had partnered him with Felicia on the car dealer investigation. Felicia had been spending more time with him than home with me. I was beginning to resent Jake Steele.

I grumbled, and Felicia said, "Besides, I thought you were hurt. Look at you. You can barely walk. You're hardly in any shape for making whoopee."

I had to admit it was true. I gave her the short version of how Haywood hired me and how I sniffed along the trail until I turned up Andrew Rollins.

"The sports doctor?"

"You know him?" Sometimes, I think Felicia knows everybody in Albuquerque.

"Not personally. Heard of him, though. Very popular with the country club set. It's become a status symbol to

have Rollins design your physical therapy after you tear up
some ligaments or whatever."

"I feel like I could use some physical therapy myself."

"You still haven't told me exactly what happened to
you."

I told her about bluffing my way into seeing Rollins and
how Ed Salisbury had shown me the door.

"The Ed Salisbury?"

"You know him, too?"

"Damn, Bubba, what do you do when I'm at work all
day? Don't you read the papers?"

I started to say something about how she works all
night, too, but thought better of it. She wasn't done anyway.

"Ed Salisbury used to play in the NFL. They called him
'Mystery Meat.' You know, like Salisbury steak? School cafe-
teria? We ran a story about him a few months ago. He's
some kind of local exercise guru. Women line up in their
leotards for a chance to sweat with him."

I muttered something about how I must've missed the
Gazette that day.

"You've really got to pay better attention, Bubba. If you'd
known Salisbury worked there, you might've handled it
differently."

"Yeah, I might've called Rollins from the safety of
another state."

Felicia had tugged on a pair of Levi's while we were talking and she took a turquoise bowling shirt off a hanger and
slipped it on. It was three sizes too big and hung on her like
bad drapes. Now she looked like my wife again.

"Could you bring me that clipping about Salisbury?" I
asked. "Maybe anything on Rollins, too?"

She nodded. Sometimes, it helps having a wife in the

newspaper business.

She opened her purse and and pulled stuff out and shoved it into her pockets—keys, change, lighter, lipstick, a slim wallet that contained her credit cards and ID. Lastly, she fished out a pack of Virginia Slims. She lipped one out before stuffing the pack in her shirt pocket.

She lit the cigarette and huffed smoke toward the ceiling. "I've got to go."

"But you just got here. Shouldn't you eat something?"

"Jake said he'd pick up Chinese takeout. We'll eat at our desks."

"Jake again. I'm really starting to dislike this guy, and I haven't even met him."

"You're going to get your chance. We're invited to his house for an office party on Saturday night."

I groaned.

"You might as well calm down," she said. "There's no getting out of it. Besides, I want to see where he lives. He inherited some kind of big old house in The Manor when his parents died."

"The Manor, huh? I'm getting tired of The Manor."

"Well, you'll be there again on Saturday. It's a command performance."

I tried to bow, but my back was too stiff to make it over very far. "Your command is my wish, your highness."

"Funny. Look, I hate to run off like this, but I really am late."

"For your Chinese food with Jake."

She frowned at me, but didn't rise to the bait.

"You don't look so good," she said instead. "Are you going to be all right?"

"I'll be fine. Just a little stiff. Lost a few quarts of blood."

"Okay then, I'd better split. Don't wait up. I could be working most of the night."

She gave me a peck on the mouth and hustled off. I limped along in her wake, but by the time I reached the living room, the front door was already closing behind her. I heard the engine of her Toyota start up before I made it to the porch to wave good-bye.

Damn. I missed my wife. I'd be glad when this special project was finished. Of course, I knew how a reporter's life really works. After the project appeared in the paper, there would be follow-ups. And court battles. And, from the sound of it, some indictments of car dealers by the state attorney general. Felicia would be busy for months to come.

I've been pretty busy myself, I thought as I stretched out on the sofa. I could use a nap.

Seven

I awoke well after ten the next morning, still on the sofa, a blanket thrown over me. I tried to sit up, but someone had poured concrete through my veins during the night. I couldn't move. The blanket seemed to indicate Felicia had come home sometime during the night and covered me up. I weakly called her name a few times. No answer.

A note was propped on the coffee table. It said, in Felicia's scrawl: "Gone back to office after a few hours' sleep. Hope you're feeling better today. Coffee's in kitchen."

Another mystery solved. Not that it would've been too difficult to guess that Felicia was working again with Jake freaking Steele. Her note left only one question for me: How was I supposed to get up off the couch to get that coffee?

I lay there a long time, slowly flexing stiff joints and sore muscles. Finally, the call of the bladder wouldn't let me lie still any longer. I forced myself up off the sofa, grunting and whimpering, and shuffled to the bathroom.

I washed my face and brushed my teeth and took more aspirin, as much for my hangover as for my aching body. I slowly made my way to the kitchen.

After a few slugs of coffee, I started to feel more awake. Usually, I start my day with coffee and the morning *Gazette*, but I was in no shape to go out into the yard to see which shrub the paperboy had thrown it under this morning. Felicia keeps a radio on the kitchen counter, always tuned to an all-news station, and I decided that would have to do. I flipped it on before I eased into a chair at the kitchen table.

The news was the usual hoo-hah about crime and punishment and traffic snarls and I wasn't paying much attention until the ruby-throated announcer ballyhooed "our top story of the hour."

"A well-known Albuquerque doctor was found slain at his office this morning. Andrew Rollins—"

I spilled coffee in my lap. It was hot.

"—was killed in a workout room at his sports medicine clinic near Downtown. Police say Rollins apparently was bludgeoned with a dumbbell. There were no witnesses, but investigators are interviewing everyone who was at the busy clinic this morning."

I got to my feet, glaring at the radio.

"Reporters are being kept out of the clinic for now, but we'll have more details as soon as the police release them. Meanwhile, in Santa Fe—"

I switched the radio off. Good God. Rollins was dead.

I hurried into the living room as fast as my aching knees would carry me and snatched up the phone. I had Melvin Haywood's card in my wallet, but my wallet wasn't in my pocket. I dug around in the sofa cushions until I found it, then called his office.

"Good morning. MHC Associates." It was the same cheerful receptionist who'd connected me to Haywood the afternoon before. I asked to speak to him and she said, "I'm sorry, but Mr. Haywood is not in the office this morning."

"Where is he?" I demanded.

"Excuse me?"

"I need to speak to him right away. It's urgent. Do you know whether he's at home?"

"May I ask who's calling?"

"My name's Bubba Mabry. I talked to him yesterday afternoon?"

"Oh, yes, Mr. Mabry, I remember you. I'm sorry, but I couldn't say whether Mr. Haywood is at home. I couldn't give out his number anyway."

"I've got the number. I'll see if I can catch him there."

I started to hang up, but she was still talking.

"It's funny. He called this morning and said he wouldn't be coming in to work. That's not like him at all."

"Did he say why?"

"I probably shouldn't say. I don't even know who you are."

"I'm a private investigator, doing some work for Mr. Haywood. That's why I need him so quickly."

"Really?" Her voice rose, and I grimaced. Another Mannix fan. "Well, maybe it would be all right to tell you then. He said he was going on vacation. Isn't that odd? Just out of the blue like that? Mr. Haywood never takes vacations. I've been here eight years and I can't remember him ever going away on a trip."

I got a sinking feeling in my stomach.

I thanked the receptionist and disconnected. I tried Haywood's home number, and an answering machine picked up after four rings. I left a message, but my heart wasn't in it. I hadn't expected him to be home. And I didn't believe he was on vacation either.

I had a pretty good idea what had happened to him. The tortoise-like accountant was on the run.

Eight

A hot shower loosened up my sore muscles. Fresh clothes felt good, too. But those were only physical improvements. Mentally, emotionally, I felt like hell. Rollins was dead, and I was pretty sure I was to blame.

The crime scene was about what you'd expect: Yellow tape strung around the parking lot. Squad cars and the Mobile Crime Lab—a converted Winnebago—parked haphazardly. A handful of bored cops standing guard. A couple of plainclothes types interviewing patients on crutches and women in workout togs. The aroma of doughnuts hanging in the air.

I parked the Ram and hobbled over to the nearest uniformed cop. He was a burly young guy with a crewcut and Terminator sunglasses and he didn't look as if he wanted to be bothered. It was nearly lunchtime and the desert sun beat down on the parking lot with enough force to eliminate anyone's cool.

"Yeah?" A fine greeting from one of the city's finest.

"Hi, my name's Mabry. I think I may have some infor—"

"Bubba!" The shout came from close behind me and I nearly jumped out of my skin.

I wheeled around to find Lieutenant Steve Romero.

Romero wore his usual guayabera shirt and knowing smile. I moaned and rolled my eyes.

"How come," I asked, "every time I know something about a homicide, you're the one in charge?"

"I was just asking myself that question. Maybe it's because I handle all the homicides in this town."

"You do not."

"Feels like it sometimes. Guess I'm just lucky to get the ones where you show up."

Romero's a straight-shooter, and he's treated me all right when our paths have crossed in the past. I even think of him as a friend, though he'd probably deny it, and he was best man when I married Felicia. He's a big square man with short black hair and a Clark Kent jawline and thick hands that look like they could bend steel. I think he's got X-ray vision, too. He's always able to see through me.

That fact didn't make it any easier to drum up a plausible story for my connection to Rollins' murder, but Romero jerked his head toward the clinic and I followed him inside. The air-conditioning felt wonderful and I took several deep breaths, trying to remain cool and calm.

"Let me guess," Romero said, sizing me up. "You've come to confess."

"What?"

"You mean you didn't kill the doc?"

"Shit, no. Where did you get that idea?"

Romero grinned. I could tell he wasn't serious about pinning the murder on me, but my skin still crawled. Suddenly, the sweat on my face felt icy.

He fished in one of the guayabera shirt's four pockets and came up with my crumpled business card. He held it out to show me. I think I winced.

"You were here yesterday, hot to see Dr. Rollins. Made something of a scene?"

"Did not. I was just trying to get a few minutes of his time. His people made the scene. That big guy, Mystery Meat, tossed me out of here."

I twisted my arm around to show Romero the bandage on my elbow. "I probably should've called a cop, had him charged with assault and battery."

"He thinks we ought to charge you with murder."

"*What?*"

"Your name came up when I asked him about suspects. He thought it was awful fishy that you were here yesterday, accusing Rollins of screwing some dead woman, and then this morning Rollins turns up dead."

I glanced around the waiting room to see who was listening. A plainclothes cop interviewed an older woman who had her arm in a sling, but she could barely answer his questions for eavesdropping on my conversation with Romero. Two uniformed cops stood near the door to the inner offices, grinning over my discomfort.

"Would I have come here voluntarily if I had something to do with it?" I asked Romero, my voice lowered.

"You don't have anything to do with it?

"Maybe I do, but I didn't kill him. I was asleep on my sofa when he was killed."

"Got any witnesses?"

I sputtered before I could squeeze out an answer. "Felicia was home at some point. I don't know exactly when she left for work, but she'd vouch for me."

"Are you sure about that? I mean, if she's making you sleep on the sofa—

"No, no. It's not like that. I just—"

The wicked grin slipped across Romero's face again. I sometimes have trouble telling when he's yanking my chain, but that grin gave it away. I took a deep breath.

"Look, do you want to hear what I know or do you just want to stand around here, making me feel foolish?"

Romero cocked an eyebrow, like he was thinking it over. Then he said, "Tell me what you have, Bubba."

So I told him: Getting hired by Melvin Haywood, being tipped that Rollins was the one who'd had the affair with Eileen, visiting Rollins' office to ask him about it. I finished with the part about Ed Salisbury giving me the heave-ho into the parking lot.

"That's it?"

"Yep."

"Didn't you tell Haywood what you'd found out?"

"Oh. Yeah, I did. I called him yesterday afternoon. Told him I wasn't certain Rollins was the guy, but he seemed satisfied that the doctor was the guilty party. I guess Rollins was something of a wolf. Even Haywood knew that much."

"But he hadn't suspected Rollins before?"

"He didn't know who it was. That's why he hired me."

"And you told him it was Rollins and then somebody bashed Rollins' brains out with a ten-pound dumbbell."

"I told him it could be Rollins, but I had some more checking to do."

"Looks like your client didn't want to wait."

"What do you mean?"

"Come on, Bubba. You tell the jealous husband the doctor poked his wife and then somebody kills the doctor and you don't suspect your client?"

Of course I did. That's why I'd come here. My shoulders sagged and I nodded.

"I made Haywood promise he wouldn't try to get revenge against the guy. But it doesn't look good, does it?"

Romero's head swiveled on his thick neck.

"This is just the kind of situation I'm always warning you about, Bubba. You've got to think about the consequences of your actions. Anybody else in your position would've made sure Rollins was the guy *before* he told the client. And then you should've made damned sure Haywood would stick to his promise."

I nodded. All this had occurred to me in the shower.

"You'd have to see this guy Haywood," I said. "He looks like a turtle. Little meek guy. Last guy in the world you'd expect to get violent."

Romero rolled his eyes. "He's meek, huh? And that was good enough for you. It's not like a meek person ever killed somebody."

"C'mon, Steve. I feel bad enough already. First I targeted Rollins for Haywood. Now, I'm targeting Haywood for you. This isn't exactly going to help me get my confidentiality badge from the Private Eye Scouts."

He didn't grin this time. That's the problem with Romero. You try to be serious, he thinks you're hilarious. You make a wisecrack and he looks at you like you pissed your pants.

A notebook had materialized in Romero's hands and I watched as he wrote down Haywood's name. He asked me for an address and I told him.

"But I don't think he's there," I said. "I called right before I came over here. Got an answering machine."

Romero looked up from the notebook to study me. "Any idea where he might be?"

I sighed. I knew we'd get to this question, but I'd been

putting it off. Romero wasn't going to like the answer.

"A receptionist at his office said he called this morning and told her he was taking a sudden vacation."

A pained expression traveled across Romero's square face. "So he's on the run."

"That's my guess, but who knows? Maybe he really did go on vacation. He's had a hard time, grieving over his wife. Maybe he decided to get away and chew on the news that she'd slept with Rollins."

Romero squinted at me. "You really believe that?"

"It's possible, isn't it? "

"I'll put out an APB, see if we can turn him up."

"Okay. Let me know if I can help."

"I think you've probably done enough already."

He poked me in the chest with a thick finger. It hurt.

"Don't run off. I'll need to ask you some more questions. And I'll need to talk to my boss, see if he wants you charged."

"Charged? With what?"

Romero sighed and spoke slowly, like he was addressing an idiot.

"You set the whole thing up, Bubba, whether you meant to or not. If Haywood is our killer, you could easily be charged as an accessory."

"You're kidding me."

"You fingered Rollins for your client. If Haywood killed him, you're culpable."

"I feel really bad about it—"

"That may not be enough for the brass. They might want you charged. They're not nice guys like me."

"But I didn't know he was going to—"

"Shut up, Bubba. Go sit down. I'll make some calls. Then

we'll go over it again."

I tried to think quickly, but I couldn't see any way out of this mess. It wasn't like I could sprint out the door and go into hiding. Romero would track me down like a blood-hound. And he'd be pissed off as well.

"I should've stayed home on the sofa," I said.

Romero grabbed me by my injured elbow, which made me dance a little jig, and steered me over to some chairs against the wall.

"I'll be right back," he said. "You sit here and think about what a screw-up you are."

"Thanks. I'll do that."

Nine

Romero turned me loose two hours later. Nobody wanted to charge me with anything—yet. He made it clear I could still face legal action, either from the district attorney or—and this was something I hadn't even considered—from Rollins' heirs, if they filed a wrongful death suit. He made me tell the whole story twice more, and he read me my rights and used a tape recorder to capture my words. I felt guilty as hell.

But then I probably was guilty, wasn't I? I'd fingered Rollins. Now he was dead. He'd impressed me as a sleazy bastard and I hadn't been happy about the way his oversized assistant tossed me out of the clinic, but I sure as hell hadn't wanted him killed.

I was pretty busy with my own miseries, but I thought some about Melvin Haywood, too. First, I couldn't believe the mild-mannered accountant would conk Rollins with a dumbbell, no matter how obsessed and crazy and jealous he felt. Second, I worried about Haywood's disappearance. If he had gone off the deep end and bashed Rollins, he might be filled with remorse by now. He might do himself in, given enough guilt and enough rope. I just hoped the cops could locate him soon.

Without really meaning to, I drove to The Manor. I

cruised the flower-lined streets and pulled to a stop in front of Haywood's house. It looked empty. I drove another block up to Rollins' house and parked.

Normally, I'll do anything to avoid talking to grieving widows. They're not rational. They weep and wail and rend their clothes. They sometimes throw things. I didn't know how Charisse Rollins might be taking her husband's death, but I knew she kept a pistol handy. If I told her I might be responsible for her husband's death, there was a good chance I'd end up standing in line behind Rollins at the Pearly Gates. And St. Peter probably would see through my lies even better than Steve Romero.

But maybe Charisse wouldn't shoot me. Hell, considering the way she'd acted about her husband the day before, maybe she didn't even care he was dead. And she might be able to answer a question for me—whether Rollins really had an affair with Eileen Haywood. Everything seemed to hinge on that long-ago affair. Or, at least, on the resulting gossip. Gossip that I'd irresponsibly repeated. If Charisse could tell me it was true, it might salve my conscience. And it might prove useful to Melvin Haywood, if the cops decided to charge him with murder.

I inched up the curving sidewalk to the door of the Rollins mansion, muttering under my breath about how only an idiot would approach Charisse now, when her husband's body was barely cold. I forced myself to ring the doorbell.

It took her a while to answer the door, and I allowed myself to believe she wasn't home. I inhaled deeply to unleash a sigh of relief, but the door swung open and there she stood and my lungful came out: "Hi there. Remember me? Sorry to bother you again, especially at a time like this, but we need to talk."

She didn't look like your traditional grieving widow. Her eyes were puffy, sure, and her nose was red. But she wore a purple silk shirt with a ruffled front and black leather pants that fit as tight as a contact lens. Her feet were bare, and her toenails were painted the same shade of purple as her loose blouse. Her hair was hidden beneath a black scarf she'd tied around her head, and she held another one of those tall, frosty rum drinks in her hands. All in all, she looked like a moll on a pirate ship.

She glowered as I stood there babbling, and I was awfully glad she wasn't armed.

"This is a bad time," she said finally. She sounded a little slurry. I guessed the drink wasn't her first of the day.

"I'm really sorry about your loss. But I need some information about your husband."

She shook her head mutely and slowly pushed the door closed. Just before it clicked shut, I blurted, "It might help catch his killer."

The door swung open again. "What did you say?"

"If I could just talk to you for a few minutes? You might have information that would help the police catch whoever killed Dr. Rollins."

"I don't know anything."

"You don't know that you do. But you might know something that you don't realize you know and that knowledge could help."

She looked confused. I didn't blame her. I hadn't tracked all that very well myself.

"Just give me five minutes. I'll ask a few questions and then I'll leave you alone."

She turned away from the door without saying anything.

I followed her inside, leaving the door open in case I had to escape. The living room looked just as it had before, except that a bottle of rum and another empty glass stood on the coffee table. Charisse, it appeared, had been pouring it down since she got the news about her husband. Not that I blamed her. Bad news like that often makes people want to crawl into a bottle. But, damn, her husband had only been dead a few hours. She should be grieving, weeping, maybe making funeral arrangements. Instead, she was tying on a queen-sized drunk. Was she drowning her sorrows or celebrating?

She sat on the fat sofa in the same place as she had the day before. She stripped the scarf off her head and shook out her blond hair. She waved the scarf at a chair opposite her and I perched on it. I was wringing my hands and I forced myself to stop it and put my hands on my knees. I suppose I looked as if I might spring to my feet any second and sprint for the door. Believe me, such thoughts were running through my head.

"Look," I began, "I feel responsible for what's happened and I want to make it right."

One eyebrow rose up her forehead. "How's that?"

I hesitated. She took another slug out of the tall glass, not taking her eyes off me.

"Remember when I was by here yesterday, asking about Eileen Haywood?"

She stared at me. I wondered if she was too inebriated to follow what I was saying, but I pushed ahead.

"One of your neighbors—sorry, but I can't say which one—told me it might've been your husband. I mean, him and Eileen. Some years ago."

"Are you shitting me?" It seemed to me she'd had the

same reaction the day before. And that hadn't turned out so well. I talked faster.

"Maybe there's nothing to it. Just gossip, you know. And, supposedly, this happened before you met Dr. Rollins. It's not like he was stepping out on you, if you see what I mean. But maybe, when he was between wives—"

"You're a loathsome son of a bitch, aren't you?" Either my shocking news had sobered her, or she wasn't as liquored up as I'd thought. Somebody who's really drunk wouldn't be able to pronounce "loathsome," much less use it in a sentence. I didn't argue the point. Truth was, at that moment I felt like a loathsome son of a bitch.

"Listen, whether it's true or not, it might be the reason your husband was killed."

That halted whatever tirade she might've been working up. She sat back on the sofa and tilted up the drink again. I took that as a sign to continue.

"I probably shouldn't have done this, but I told Melvin Haywood about the gossip. I mean, I told him it was just that—gossip—and that he shouldn't take any action until I could get some proof. He promised me—"

"You think Melvin Haywood killed Andrew?"

I nodded. It felt bad to admit it, but Romero had already put me through the wringer with such questions. I'd reached the point where I thought I deserved whatever blame she wanted to sling my way. I just hoped her pistol was safely out of reach somewhere.

Then Charisse surprised me. She started laughing. Not just a little tee-hee either. A big old belly laugh, one that went on a long time and brought tears to her eyes. Just as I was beginning to think that she'd slipped into some kind of post-trauma hysteria, that maybe I ought to summon the guys with the butterfly nets, she got herself under control enough to say, "My God, you're an idiot."

That stung.

She carefully set her drink on the coffee table and rose unsteadily from the couch.

"Andrew never would've had an affair with Eileen. My God, they were practically the same age! You think Andrew would go for some dowdy housewife? He had better taste than that."

I opened my mouth to interject something about how lust can make people do funny things, but I couldn't get a word in.

"It's nonsense! Andrew was rich. He was sophisticated. He could have any woman he wanted. Why would he mess around with Eileen?"

I had no answer for that. After all, Rollins was a man who could marry a young looker like Charisse. Not natural that he'd go for Melvin Haywood's wife. It had seemed plausible before, when Nancy Chilton told me about it. It was easy to picture Rollins between wives, feeling a little lonely. And there was Eileen, stuck at home all day while Melvin worked. I had imagined her lured into an affair by the debonair doctor. But did it make sense?

"And you think Melvin Haywood, little Melvin, might've killed Andrew?" Charisse continued. "That's even more ridiculous."

She teetered across the room to where an intercom box hung on the wall. She pushed the button and said, "Ed? Can you come in here please?"

Ed? My heart skipped a beat. Couldn't be Ed Salisbury, could it? Not the same Ed who'd hurled me across a parking lot like a Frisbee. No way Mystery Meat would be here when cops still were swarming over the clinic.

I didn't get a chance to sort it all out. Charisse swiveled around to face me, and I felt I should give her my full attention.

"Melvin Haywood couldn't hurt a flea," she said. "And he's smart, too. I can't believe he would listen to this nonsense about Andrew and Eileen. Of course, it doesn't seem possible that a smart man like him would hire an idiot like you either."

"Hey now—" I was a little tired of being called an idiot. I had my own doubts about Melvin's killer instinct and my own detecting abilities, but all this name-calling wasn't helping.

Ed Salisbury lumbered around a corner into the living room. He was so big, he looked like he could block out the sun, form his own eclipse. My bowels turned to Jell-O and my feet danced. Mystery Meat's face doubled on itself as he scowled at me.

"What the hell are you doing here?"

I tried to answer, but my throat had closed up. Charisse Rollins did all the talking.

"He thinks Melvin Haywood killed Andrew. He told Melvin that Andrew had an affair with Eileen, and now he thinks Melvin killed him. Can you believe it?"

Mystery Meat seemed to cross the room in a single bound. He stood over me, his fists on his hips, glaring down at me. He looked like Mr. Clean's hairy brother. I tried to squeeze into the cushions of the chair, but they would only give so far.

"The doc said he didn't do it," Meat said. "I was there when you asked him about it. He said it was bullshit. And now you're here, telling his widow that same trash?"

"I know it seems—"

He popped me on top of the head with an open palm. It was like getting whacked with a two-by-four. The impact made me bite my tongue, which probably was just as well. I'd already talked myself into plenty of trouble. My tongue deserved biting.

"Get the hell out of here," he said.

I tried to obey, but my knees were rubbery and he loomed so close, there really wasn't room to stand without bumping into his brawny chest. Didn't matter anyway. Salisbury wouldn't patiently stand by while I slinked out of the house. He grabbed my hair and lifted me to my feet. I whimpered. Once I was standing, I thought about trying to punch him in the stomach, distract him for a second so I could flee. But I probably would've just broken my hand on his Abs of Steel.

He spun me around and marched me toward the front door, his big hands holding tight to my shirt.

The heavy oak door still stood open, or he might've pushed my head through it. I felt myself lift off the ground and then I was flying through the air. I had one random thought: If I keep doing this much flying, I'm going to earn my wings.

I hit the flagstone sidewalk on all fours and bounced into a flower bed. I sprawled there on my back, damp soil seeping into my pants, my head spinning as pain clamored for my attention. Salisbury stood over me and his breath was coming hard and, I couldn't help myself, I looked down at his giant sneakers, expecting them to stomp me into mulch. He seemed to consider that plan, but caught himself and exhaled loudly.

"Don't come around here again," he said, his voice

thick. And then he turned and stalked back into the house. The big door slammed.

And there I sat, among the posies, hurting all over. My palms were raw and my knees ached and my ego was deflated. I slowly got to my feet and brushed myself off and stumbled out to the curb where my big truck waited with its smirking chrome grille.

Ten

I was soaking in the bathtub when Felicia got home a little after five o'clock. I heard her calling my name from the living room, and I responded with a feeble, "In here."

She pushed open the bathroom door (privacy doesn't count for much with Felicia) and found me submerged in steaming water, my bruised knees sticking up like icebergs.

"What are you doing?"

This seemed like a silly question, but I wasn't about to point that out to her. Besides, I knew what she meant. I almost never take baths. I got used to showers when I was living in cheap motels. Anyhow, it only took her a second more to scope out the red and purple that decorated my kneecaps.

"What happened to you?"

I sat up, my hair and chin dripping water. The sudden air against my chest felt cold, even though it was hot July outside and our house's thrumming cooler wasn't doing much good on the inside. I crossed my arms over my chest before I answered.

"I got tossed out of another building," I muttered.

She looked cross. "Another giant?"

"Same one."

She huffed and rolled her eyes and fished a cigarette out

of her pocket. She took her time lighting it, and I figured she was using the moment to cook up her latest jab at my inadequacies in the private eye field. Instead, she asked, "Are you hurt bad?"

"No worse than yesterday. Just new bruises and scrapes in different places."

I held up my scraped hands like a supplicant. She leaned over to look, squinting against her own smoke.

"You'll live," she pronounced as she straightened up. "But I'd quit messing around with old Mystery Meat, if I were you."

I shook my head, sending a fine spray around the bathroom.

"I wasn't messing with him. I didn't even know he was there. I went to see Rollins' widow and Salisbury appeared out of nowhere and tossed me into the flower beds."

"Wait a minute. Did you say 'widow?'"

"Haven't you heard? Andrew Rollins turned up dead this morning."

Felicia's eyes widened. Despite all my aches and pains and guilt, I felt a little ember of satisfaction inside. I never hear news before Felicia.

"Natural causes?"

"Nope. Murdered. I take it no one told you about it."

She shook her head, looking peeved. "Somebody could've dropped The Bomb and I wouldn't have heard about it. I'm off hard news until we get this project finished."

"I thought you were nearly done."

"Getting there. We think some of these car dealers are onto us. We've been staking them out, trying to catch more of them doing their dirty deeds, but no luck so far."

I was a little unclear on what dirty deeds we were talking about, but I didn't say so. I felt sure Felicia had told me
all about it at some point in the unending conversation
that is our marriage. It's never good to appear I wasn't
paying attention. I just nodded knowingly and sank back
into the bath.

Felicia closed the lid on the toilet and sat down facing
me. She took another drag on the cigarette and said, "So
Andrew Rollins got murdered, huh?"

I nodded, got a mouthful of bath water. I spat it out
before I replied.

"Somebody brained him with a dumbbell in the gym at
his clinic. I heard about it on the radio and went over there,
only to get grilled by Steve Romero and his pals. Romero
acted like I was the one who killed Rollins."

Felicia grinned. "Good ol' Steve."

"Then I told him about my client and how we suspected Rollins was the one who had an affair with the late wife.
So now Melvin Haywood is Public Enemy Number One."

"He under arrest?"

"Last I heard, they still hadn't found him. He took a sudden 'vacation' this morning, around the time Rollins
bought the farm."

"Ouch. That doesn't look good."

"Tell me."

She stood up and lifted the lid and tossed her cigarette
into the toilet. It sizzled when it hit the water and died. I
knew exactly how it felt.

"I've got to go," she said.

"You just got here!"

"I know, Bubba, but I've still got work to do. Jake and I
have to tail another car dealer tonight. We think he's going

to be moving the paperwork on some hot cars."

Oh, yeah. Stolen cars. That's what the investigation entailed. The reporters suspected stolen cars were being driven to New Mexico, painted and otherwise altered, then sold as used cars once the paperwork had been forged to cover up the ownership trail. Felicia had told me all about it over dinner a week ago. Remembering it pleased me. You take enough whaps to the head in the course of a private eye career, you worry it'll ruin your memory. I sometimes fear I'll end up like this guy Slappy, who wanders up and down The Cruise, asking strangers, "Do you know me? Who am I?" Slappy wants to put his own picture on milk cartons.

"You going to be all right?" Felicia asked.

"Yeah. I'm soaking out some of the aches. Then I'll dry off and put bandages all over my body."

"I'd better be going then. I just stopped by to drop off those clippings you wanted. They're on the coffee table. I don't know that you need them now. Sounds like your case left town."

I glumly agreed. She leaned over and kissed my forehead, which was one of the few places that didn't hurt. Then she was out the door and gone.

I worried about Felicia and all the time she was spending on her special project. It's not healthy to work all the time, around the clock. Especially in the company of former TV reporter Jake Steele, who was undoubtedly a handsome devil. The thought of Felicia and Jake, all cozied up in a surveillance vehicle, made me itchy. I've spent a lot of time sitting in cars, staking out motels and whatnot, and I know how lonely it can get. People can forget themselves. They glom onto the nearest friendly face, any interested ear. I wondered what Felicia and Jake talked about while they spent so much time together. I wondered what they'd say about the death of Andrew Rollins and how Felicia's screw-up husband was mixed up in it.

Which brought me back to the Rollins killing. What the hell was Ed Salisbury doing at Rollins' home only hours after the murder? He could say he was there ministering to the grieving widow, but Charisse seemed to be holding up pretty well, thanks to the rum, and Ed had been off in some other part of the house. I wondered whether Rollins had a home office. Maybe Mystery Meat had been going through papers, looking for a will.

By the time I'd mulled all this, the bath had become too chilly to tolerate and I was pruney all over. I dried off and checked my wounds in the mirror. Despite what I'd told Felicia, I didn't paste Band-Aids all over my body. My new scrapes were in places where bandages would never stay stuck anyway—my palms, my knees. I was having enough trouble moving around without taping over all my joints. The scab on my elbow had gone soft and yucky in the bath, so I decided it needed air. I gingerly slipped on my bathrobe and padded into the living room.

Photocopies of the newspaper clippings sat on the coffee table where Felicia had left them. I eased onto the sofa and read through them. She'd included a couple from Salisbury's NFL days, both of which talked about his ferocity on the football field. Apparently, he'd been a demon tackler, one of those pass rushers that give quarterbacks the night sweats. I could believe it. He was strong and mean enough in person. I couldn't imagine what he must've been like wearing pads and a helmet.

The clippings on Rollins were slim pickings. A wedding

announcement from when he married Charisse. A couple of brief items on his medical practice.

At the bottom of the stack was the feature story Felicia had mentioned the day before. It ran under a big photograph that showed Salisbury, all decked out in white, leading an exercise class at the clinic. The class was mostly women, and I couldn't see anything wrong with most of them. If they had sports injuries they were treating, they must've had them hidden under their skimpy leotards. The women glowed and smiled and they only had eyes for Meat.

The article talked about how sports medicine was a booming business. All these middle-aged "athletes" still trying to prove something, wrecking their knees and shoulders, gave Rollins and Salisbury a huge customer base. I've never understood why people place their bodies in jeopardy just to climb a mountain or throw a softball or otherwise act like children. My idea of participating in sports is to lie on the sofa, watching football on TV. Rooting for a favorite team can be aerobic, I tell myself, it can get the old heart rate up.

I keep telling myself I need to get in shape, but I don't do anything about it. It all seems unnecessary and dangerous. Of course, if I was in better shape, maybe I'd bounce back faster from being chucked around a parking lot.

A paragraph in the article described how Rollins had patched Salisbury up after he'd ruined both knees in a playoff game a decade earlier. Salisbury was quoted as saying he got so interested in the physical therapy that helped him walk again that he'd gone to school to become a therapist himself. Rollins apparently had funded the schooling with the idea that Salisbury would go to work for him when it was done. Guess the doctor foresaw that having a big, handsome athlete on the payroll would help attract patients. Not to mention that Salisbury would be handy if Rollins needed to remove any private eyes from the building.

I creaked up off the sofa and went to the kitchen. I made a sandwich and drank a couple of beers. I took some more pain relievers and limped off to bed. I lay awake a long time, wondering where Melvin Haywood was, what he was doing. And why the hell Andrew Rollins had to die.

Eleven

Friday morning, I awoke stiff and sore. It was becoming a habit. I plodded into the kitchen and gulped down hot coffee and aspirin.

No sign of Felicia. No note, nothing. Near as I could tell, she'd never come home the night before. That worried me, but before I could get too worked up, the doorbell rang.

Now let me explain something here. I have an office in my home, sure, but nobody ever visits it. I use the desk and the phone and the filing cabinets that are crammed full of old notes and documents and other disorganized crap, but I don't entertain clients there. When I need to see clients, I usually go to them or I meet them on some neutral turf like the Olympus Café. Considering how some of my cases turn out, I've always figured it was better if clients weren't too familiar with where I live. So when the doorbell rang at nine o'clock on a Friday morning, I expected a deliveryman or an Avon lady or a gang of recruiters for the Jehovah's Witnesses.

I didn't expect it to be Nancy Chilton.

She whipped off expensive-looking sunglasses when I answered the door. She wore a pale pink blouse and a white skirt that showed off her tanned legs. She had on high heels that matched her white shoulder bag. She looked very summery and together and rich. I was still wearing my bathrobe.

"Mrs. Chilton? What are you doing here?"

She had my business card in her hand and she looked down at it and then up at me and said, "I thought this was your business address."

"It is. I mean, it's my home, too. My office is through that door over there, around the side of the house."

She leaned backward to try to look around the corner to where my office entrance was set into the wall, probably had cobwebs hanging over the door. She smiled.

"Should I go around there and ring the bell? Would that give you time to put on some pants?"

My cheeks warmed. "No, come on in. You can get to my office this way, too. And I keep my pants in the other end of the house."

I showed her into my office, pointed at the gut-sprung sofa against one wall and told her to make herself at home. Then I hurried off to the bedroom to hunt up some clothes.

Getting dressed was painful, but I distracted myself by wondering what Nancy Chilton wanted and why she'd arrived unannounced. She could've called. I would've gladly stopped by her place. I seemed to spend all my time in The Manor anyhow.

I hustled back to the office in my bare feet, tucking my shirttails into the snug waistband of yesterday's jeans. She was right where I'd left her, sitting on the edge of the sofa, her feet together and her purse on her lap. I limped over to the old swivel chair at my desk and sat down to face her.

"Now, then, what can I do for you?"

She gave me the white smile again. Hard to believe such a pleasant mouth could spew such vile gossip.

"Sorry about showing up here so early," she said. "But I read about Andrew Rollins in the *Gazette* this morning and felt like I should see you right away."

I leaned toward her, careful not to rest my elbows on my bruised knees. "Do you know something about his death?"

"Nothing beyond what I told you already about Eileen. I was afraid that had something to do with Andrew's death."

I shrugged my shoulders, uncovering a fresh stab of pain near my collarbone. I think I must've winced.

"Are you all right, Bubba? You're moving kind of stiffly."

I tried to laugh it off, but I wasn't very convincing.

"Took a little spill yesterday."

She looked as if she was trying not to smile, but she didn't pursue it further. Instead, she sobered up and said, "Have you talked to Melvin since the murder?"

"Mr. Haywood suddenly went on vacation yesterday. I haven't been able to reach him."

"Really?" Her face took on a glow at this news. "But you told him about Eileen and Andrew? About their affair?"

"I told him about it, but I told him I didn't have any proof. I also made him promise to leave Dr. Rollins alone. Looks like maybe he didn't keep his promise."

"You think Melvin had him killed?"

Her manicured hands stayed busy with her purse. I couldn't tell whether she was nervous or just excited about the potential scandal. The more I said, the worse I'd make this situation. I turned the question back to her.

"What do you think? You know Haywood better than I do. Is he capable of something like that?"

Her eyes cast about my tattered office while she thought it over.

"I wouldn't have believed so. But there's no telling what people will do when they're jealous."

I nodded knowingly. Exactly what I'd been telling myself.

"Are the police looking for Melvin?" she asked. "The newspaper didn't mention him."

"I really can't say, Mrs. Chilton. I talked to the police yesterday, but it was all confidential."

A look of alarm registered on her face, but she erased it with another smile.

"You didn't mention my name to the police, did you, Bubba?"

"No, I didn't."

My own answer surprised me. I hadn't realized it at the time, but Romero hadn't asked where I'd heard the gossip about Eileen Haywood and Andrew Rollins. I'd said it had come from "a neighbor" and he hadn't pursued it any further. The omission almost made me grin. It was pretty rare that anything got past Steve Romero.

"Thank you," she said. "I so badly want to stay out of this terrible situation."

"Is that why you came to see me? To make sure I hadn't sicced the cops on you?"

She fidgeted some more. "Partly that. But I had another reason, too."

I waited her out. The way this case had gone so far, it was about time I sat quietly.

"I don't know how to begin," she began. "I've never done anything like this before."

"Like what?"

"Remember the other day, when I said I might need a private investigator some time? Well, now's the time. I want to hire you."

I couldn't have been more stunned if she'd shed her clothes and set her hair on fire.

"Hire me to do what?"

"Investigate, of course. My husband. I think he's having an affair."

I nearly fell out of my chair.

"Your husband? You want to me to build a case against your own husband? After the way I've screwed up the Haywood case?"

Now, this wasn't a good reaction to a job offer. You won't find that technique in any of those books about How to Build Your Business. But she'd pitched me such a curve, I didn't know which way to swing.

"I don't blame you for what happened to Andrew Rollins," she said. "As far as I'm concerned, Andrew brought it all on himself. If he hadn't been such a sneak and a cheat, none of this would've happened."

I could see her argument, though it wasn't very convincing. I didn't really want to get further involved with Nancy Chilton, but if she was willing to overlook my failings and send some cash my way, who was I to argue?

"Tell me all about it."

She caught herself puttering with her purse and set it on the sofa beside her. She clasped her busy hands together and leaned forward, just as she'd done when she was telling me Eileen Haywood's secrets. That memory didn't make me any more comfortable.

"For years, I've looked the other way while Boyd fooled around with younger women, but I can't do it anymore. In a way, you're responsible for my change of heart."

"Me?"

"When you came to my house and asked me about Eileen, it reminded me how she had talked me out of divorcing Boyd. And the way you described poor Melvin, so broken up over Eileen's death and her disloyalty, it made me think. Why have I put up with Boyd messing around all these years?"

An image of her big fancy home flitted through my mind, followed quickly by one of Boyd, in his cowboy hat, hawking cars on TV. I had a pretty good idea what had kept Nancy from dumping him in the past, and it involved dollar signs.

"I've decided I've had enough," she said. "There's still time to make a life for myself, one that doesn't include pacing around the house at all hours, wondering when my husband will get home."

Her face glowed crimson, with anger or embarrassment, and it seemed like a good time for the barefoot detective to get to the point.

"What makes you think he's having an affair?"

"I know all the signs. He comes home late. He showers before coming to bed so I won't smell her on him. He makes excuses about going out of town on business. It's all lies, all of it. I know he's seeing a woman."

"And you want proof."

She sat back. Her knuckles had gone white where her hands were clasped together.

"It would help, wouldn't it? When I march him into divorce court? I want to take the son of a bitch for everything he's got."

"Divorces don't really work that way in this state."

"Of course, it won't ever get to court," she continued, and she seemed to be talking to herself as much as to me. "Once he knows I've got the goods on him, he'll settle and he'll settle big. He wouldn't want his infidelities to get into the newspaper. Car dealers already have enough image problems."

She was right about that. Nobody trusts car dealers. And their image was about to take another hit, as soon as Felicia and Jake Steele got their stories done.

I picked up a pen and pad from my desktop and asked her more questions about Boyd's habits and her suspicions. She told me she thought her husband had stopped having affairs for a time. The Chiltons had one daughter, Amy, and Boyd had seemed to settle down when Amy was in high school. But once the daughter went off to college back East, he'd started up again. Showing up late, making excuses.

"I think he's meeting this woman tonight."

"Tonight?"

"He told me this morning, as he was leaving for work, that he'd be late coming home. Business, he said. On a Friday night. Who does he think he's fooling? I want you to follow him when he leaves the dealership. See if he doesn't go running off to some little filly. Then I want you to get my proof."

"Photos?"

"However you usually handle such things."

"Usually I take pictures. Sometimes, that's sort of hard for the wife."

"Believe me, Bubba, anything you turn up won't hold a candle to what I've imagined he's been up to all these years."

I hesitated. Did I want to work for Nancy Chilton? Did I want to get further involved in the soap opera that was life in The Manor? But then Nancy made up my mind for me. She said the magic words as she reached for her purse.

"I suppose you'll need a retainer? I'll just write you a check."

Twelve

By late afternoon, I was glad I had the Chilton case to pursue. Nothing else was working out. Andrew Rollins was still dead. Melvin Haywood was still unavailable for comment. Lieutenant Steve Romero still suspected that Haywood and I somehow had cooked up the doctor's death. I still was sore all over. And Felicia still hadn't come home. I was happy to do a simple tail job to see if Boyd Chilton was stepping out on his wife. At least that was something I understood.

Boyd Chilton Motors sat along Lomas Boulevard east of downtown and north of the university, in a row of auto dealerships that feed on the traffic pouring off Interstate 25. It wasn't the easiest place to do surveillance. The main building, housing the offices and the garage and body shop, squatted at the back of the lot, nestled under a hill that rose to vacant land owned by UNM. Between the building and Lomas were acres of sticky asphalt and rows of shiny cars, some with balloons tethered to their antennas.

No way my dusty truck would disappear among all those new autos. And I didn't dare set foot on the lot. A dozen salesmen would swoop down on me like vultures if I showed the least interest in a new vehicle.

I drove through the lot once, drawing eager looks from

circling salesmen. Behind the office, an employees' parking lot was squeezed between the building and the eroded
face of the hill. The lot had a chainlink gate and Nancy
Chilton had warned me I'd need a card-key to get in there.
I sat in my truck, staring at the gate, trying to work something out, long enough that one of the sweaty salesmen
headed my way. Then I got an idea and drove off before he
could reach me.

I turned south on University Boulevard, went up the
steep hill, then took the first right onto a street called Mesa
Vista. Two-story sorority houses sat on either side of the
street behind jade lawns, and the street ended just beyond
them. It widened enough to allow cars to turn around and
go out again, but I had another idea.

Beyond the cul-de-sac was bare dirt studded with tufts
of sun-bleached grass. The dirt was tamped down from stu-
dents parking there illegally. I eased the Ram up over the
curb and let it lumber over packed ruts until I was near the
spot where the hill dropped down to Chilton Motors. I
jockeyed the truck around so I could see the employees'
parking lot below.

I spotted Chilton's car, a long gold Cadillac nudged up to
the back door of the dealership. I sat in the comfort of my
truck and watched the lot, running my air conditioner
occasionally to keep from slipping into heat stroke and
sometimes whipping my head around to get the crick out
of my neck.

I was there about an hour and my aspirin wore off and
I was feeling achy and hot and itchy. I kept expecting a
patrol car from the UNM police department to roll up and
run me off school property. It almost would've been a relief.

Then Boyd Chilton stepped through the back door. He

wore a huge white cowboy hat, just like the one he wore in his TV commercials. He turned to say something to somebody inside the dealership, which gave me a moment to study him. He wore a brown, western-cut suit over a white shirt with an open collar. Shiny cowboy boots. He was around fifty pounds overweight, most of it stored in a paunch that pulled his shirt tight. He turned back toward me as he fished in his pocket for his keys. The cowboy hat shaded his eyes, but I could see a pug nose and red jowls framed by wide, grizzled sideburns.

He unlocked the Cadillac's door and flung it open. Then he carefully removed the hat from his head before sliding behind the wheel. That's when I saw the hat was more than a prop. Boyd Chilton's head was shiny-bald on the top and he sported a nice sunburn. His head looked like a red doorknob. Then he was behind the wheel and exhaust spouted from the Cadillac's tailpipe. I cranked up the Ram and bumped toward the street.

I caught up with Chilton just as he turned north onto University Boulevard. It was rush hour, but that big gold Caddie was easy to spot and a snap to tail.

We followed University past offices and warehouses and buildings owned by UNM. The road went through a big "S" curve as it dipped below I-40, the main east-west route through the Sun Belt, and there were motels and the giant truck stop where my father, Dub, sometimes lands his semi when he's roaring across the country. North of the truck stop, University melds with the frontage roads for northbound I-25. I followed the Cadillac onto the busy freeway.

Boyd Chilton had a heavy foot. The Caddie roared off at seventy-five miles per hour, and it was all I could do to keep from losing him. I always drive near the speed limit because I have a problem with authority figures. Getting stopped for a speeding ticket can turn me into a babbling wreck. But I didn't want to lose Chilton in the thick traffic. I hadn't done much right lately, and I wanted this tail to be a success.

Fortunately, we only traveled a few miles at warp speed before Chilton signaled he was exiting the freeway at San Antonio Avenue. I was right behind him on the exit ramp. If he noticed me on his bumper, he didn't let on. He seemed intent on getting somewhere in a hurry, and that made my heart beat faster. Old Boyd was rushing around like a horny man on his way to a rendezvous.

The north end of Albuquerque has grown like crazy in the past few years. I've lived here long enough to remember when the area was sand and scrub and jackrabbits. Now, office towers and apartment complexes and fancy homes crowd along streets that were dirt tracks when I first came to the city eighteen years ago. The area has a treeless, dusty feel to it, like it's still one big construction zone. Scrub and sand have been replaced by asphalt and concrete. I don't know what happened to the jackrabbits.

San Antonio is now a smooth four-lane and Chilton drove east at a good clip. I hung back, keeping him in sight while worrying over my speed. We passed a parked patrol car at one point and I let off the gas and coasted past, glancing sidelong to see if the cop was working radar. He had a clipboard resting against his steering wheel, busy with paperwork. Chilton didn't even give him a look. Guess if you're a big wheel, you don't worry about speeding tickets. Hell, Boyd probably could afford to wallpaper his house in citations.

The Cadillac slowed and swung into the parking lot of a big stucco stockade called the Alamo Arms. I crept along, not wanting to be spotted, and rounded a corner of a building just as Boyd Chilton got out of the Cadillac. He waddled toward Apartment 122. I drove on past without gazing his way, so I don't know if he gave me a second look. I stopped at the next corner, watching my mirrors, and saw Chilton knock on the door. I threw the Ram into reverse and backed into a parking space that left me facing the apartment.

I only got a glimpse of the woman who opened the door, but she was young and raven-haired and scantily clad and she threw her arms around Chilton's beefy neck as the door swung closed behind him.

I waited a while before I got out of the truck. I figured I'd give them time to have a beer, engage in some small talk and shuck their clothes before I tried to peek in the windows.

The sun still was high in the sky. I didn't much like the idea of prowling around the apartment complex in broad daylight, particularly at a time when people were arriving home from work. But I didn't see how I had much choice. Boyd and his chippy didn't appear to be going out for the evening, and he didn't look like the kind of Lothario who could do the horizontal bop all night long. Better to catch them in the act, before it was all over.

I got my camera bag from behind the seat of the Ram and took out my little Nikon and checked that it had fresh film. The compact camera was great to use during cool weather because it was small enough to fit into the pocket of a jacket. This being July, I wasn't wearing a jacket. My polo shirt didn't have a pocket at all. I cupped the camera in one hand and held it against my belly as I strolled toward Boyd's love nest.

What property wasn't taken up by the apartment buildings was mostly given over to parking. A strip of grass wide enough for one swath of a mower separated the buildings from the sidewalk. Against the buildings grew prickly evergreen shrubs, aimed at keeping people away from the windows.

I circled the building Chilton had entered, figuring the bedrooms were on the back side, away from the parking lot. The rear of the woman's apartment was mostly blank stucco, but good-sized windows were cut into the walls at waist height. Miniblinds covering one of the windows were part way open and I could see right into the bedroom. I pressed against the wall and looked around. The building backed up to another building arranged the same way. The shades were closed in the windows across from me. The grassy alley between the buildings was a sort of no-man's land, and I figured I was safe from prying eyes while I did my peeping and photographing.

I crouched and duck-walked into the narrow gap between the shrubs and the wall. I peered around the edge of the window and found myself looking right at Boyd Chilton. He was naked except for pink boxer shorts and was sitting on the edge of the bed maybe six feet from the window. The girl—she couldn't have been more than twenty-two years old—was on her knees behind him, kneading his shoulders. Boyd had his eyes closed and a big grin on his face. The girl's eyes were open, but she wasn't looking my way. She was looking down at Boyd's bald head, as if she could see her reflection there. The smile on her face was sort of dreamy and I wondered whether she was high on something, or if she truly enjoyed making whoopee with fat, bald men. Maybe there was hope for me yet.

I slipped the Nikon up to my face and snapped off a quick one through the blinds. I wasn't sure the camera was getting much of a shot. The slats were tilted and it was pretty dim inside. The sunlight falling through the blinds put stripes of shade over everything in the room. The girl started kissing Chilton's fat neck, which gave me the creeps, but I fired off another frame or two, saving most of the film for what was to come.

You witness a lot of ugly stuff when you're a private eye. I've seen my share of corpses and bloodshed, dirty dealings and drug addicts, cheaters and teasers. But I can honestly say I've never seen anything quite as nauseating as this boar hog hugging up his lithe young sweetie. I didn't see how she could stand it. It must've been like taking a bath in sweat, using Boyd for a blubbery sponge. But she didn't seem to mind his bulk or his perspiration or the fact he was wearing pink boxer shorts. She might've been a pro, accustomed to ignoring the immediate circumstances of her job, keeping focused on the money to come. But I have to say she seemed to enjoy herself as she shimmied out of her teddy and pressed her bare breasts up against the car dealer.

I shot more pictures, which was difficult considering that I was making a face the whole time. Boyd crawled on the bed behind the woman and bent her over and I figured this was the money shot. I could see both of their faces, so intent on their doggy-style lovemaking. In the pictures, there would be no doubt about what they were doing.

Maybe I got a little too eager. I shifted my position so I

was more fully in front of the window, trying to get both of their faces in the same frame.

The woman opened her eyes and looked right at me. Her mouth made an "O" of surprise and then her lips started moving rapidly. I couldn't make out what she was saying through the window, but Boyd didn't have any trouble hearing her. He saw me, too, and he rolled off the bed and grabbed at his boxer shorts, which were down around his knees.

I shot a few more frames as Boyd hitched up his boxers and the woman screamed and grabbed at the bedclothes to cover herself. Then I realized Boyd wasn't trying to hide. He pulled on his cowboy boots and headed for the apartment's front door. Uh-oh. Time to hit the road.

I scrambled through the low shrubs and took off for my truck, skirting the edge of the building, running in the strip of clipped grass. The front of the apartment was between me and the Ram, and there was a good chance I'd run right into Chilton if I didn't hurry.

I was making good time, lifting my knees, pumping my elbows, holding the camera in one hand. The apartment door flung open and Boyd came puffing out onto the front stoop, still wearing only his boxer shorts and cowboy boots. I cut right, just to make sure he couldn't get to me, but I knew I was home free. It was only forty feet to where I'd left the truck. I might not be in good shape and I might be stiff all over from my run-ins with Mystery Meat, but I could outrun fat Boyd that far. I leaped off the curb onto the asphalt parking lot just as I heard his angry shout—"Hey!"

Maybe I glanced back at him over my shoulder. I really don't remember. All I know is that I came down funny on the asphalt and turned my left ankle. Lost my balance. I stumbled forward a few paces, windmilling my arms, trying to regain my equilibrium.

And the camera went flying out of my hand.

It soared through the air, tumbling end over end, and hit the pavement with a clatter. Its door opened as it skittered across the asphalt, exposing the film, and bits of lens scattered like spilled diamonds.

I made a sound like this: "Gawaaaaah!"

Pain shot up my leg and I hopped around on one foot, still trying to get my balance. If I fell, it would be all over. Boyd Chilton would set on me like a junkyard dog.

No time to retrieve the camera, which looked beyond repair anyway. I hopped and skipped and hitched my way to the Ram and threw myself behind the wheel.

Chilton had closed the gap pretty well, his boots slapping the sidewalk. He was close enough that I hit the door lock before I put the key in the ignition. He was banging on my window when a Ford turned into the parking lot, headed our way. Some poor schmuck, coming home from work, only to find: 1) a fat man in pink boxers puffing like the big, bad wolf, 2) a terrified guy with a sickly pallor behind the wheel of a red truck, and 3) a shattered camera on the pavement. The car did the trick, though. Boyd suddenly recognized he was out in public in his underwear.

He froze. Looked down at himself. Hesitated.

I started the truck. Boyd glanced from me to the approaching car and back again. His face was bright red with anger and exertion. With his bald head and his round cheeks, he looked like a baby in the middle of a tantrum.

I threw the truck into gear and steered away from him.

Seeing there was no way to get to me, Chilton took what

spoils he could manage. I watched in my mirror as he bent over and snatched up the broken camera. He straightened and waved it at me. The middle finger of his other hand was aimed my way. His mouth was moving, but I couldn't hear him. Just the roar of the Ram's engine and my own pulse pounding in my head.

Boyd held the camera up to shield his face from the other car, which had braked to a stop beyond. The guy behind the wheel made me think of Mickey Mouse. His face was three black circles—the lenses of his sunglasses and his open mouth. Boyd hurried away.

And me? I went home to lick my wounds. My ankle throbbing, my head pounding and my ego badly maimed. I'd blown the case, ruined the photos, lost my camera.

And I got a speeding ticket on the freeway on the way home.

Thirteen

I was in such a bad mood when I pulled into my drive-way, even the sight of Felicia's car didn't cheer me. I limped into the house and found her in the kitchen.

She was wearing her nightgown. It's not exactly a slinky number, nothing like the lacy teddy Boyd's girlfriend had been wearing, but it's a nightgown nonetheless and I certainly didn't expect to find her dressed that way when the sun was still up outside. Her hair was mussed and there were circles under her eyes and she wasn't wearing her glasses. She looked as if she'd just rolled out of bed, or was about to roll into one.

Now, listen, I trust my wife. She's an honest person, loyal and true. But I'd just come from the scene of a grave infidelity, Boyd and his little miss having the time of their lives before they were interrupted by a window-peeper. Seeing such things destroys whatever small faith one has in mankind and marriage and commitment. Then to come home and find one's spouse in her bedclothes, well, let's just say it was unsettling.

"What's the matter with you?" She squinted at me, try-ing to focus.

"What do you mean?"

"You're limping."

"Oh, that. Turned my ankle. No big deal."

"What did you think I meant?"

"Um, I don't know." Stall. No way she could've read my expression from across the room. Not without her glasses.

She had a glass of water in her hand and she knocked down some aspirin.

"Are you sick?" I asked.

She shook her head. "Just a headache."

I sighed in relief. If she had a headache, I had no reason to worry. It wasn't like I'd find some guy hiding in the closet. I know the "I've-got-a-headache" excuse is a lame cliché, but I've learned there's truth to it, as there is with most clichés. There's no getting amorous with Felicia when she's got a headache, not unless you want your own head handed to you.

"I'm beat," she said. "I haven't had any sleep in thirty-six hours."

"So that's why you're in your nightgown?"

"Of course."

"I thought maybe you'd already been to bed and were just getting up or something. You never came home last night, right?"

She shook her head. "Sorry, I should've called. I kept thinking I'd get to go home soon and then, by the time I saw it was going to be all night, it was too late to call. Hope you didn't worry."

"No, that's fine," I lied. "What were you doing all night?"

"Jake and I followed this idiot we thought was moving some of the fake paperwork on those hot cars. The guy never set his briefcase down for a second. He's going to bars and visiting friends and always he's carrying the briefcase.

We kept thinking, if we could only get a peek inside there—"

"You followed this guy all night long?"

"Not all night. Even car thieves have to sleep. And once Jake figured out what was in the briefcase, we were done anyway. But it was well after midnight and we decided to pull an all-nighter. We were at the newsroom, cross-referencing notes and checking stuff on the computer the rest of the time."

I mulled all this while I limped over to the sofa and flopped down. I propped my throbbing foot up on the coffee table.

"What was it?" I asked.

"What was what?"

"In the briefcase. What was in the briefcase?"

"Oh, that. Cocaine."

"The guy's selling cocaine?"

"Just a user. Jake said he had a bag full of powder and he'd open it up and stick his head down behind the top of the briefcase to get a snort."

"And how did Jake find this out?"

"He followed him into a men's room. Heard him sniffing and snorting in a stall. Jake peeked through the slit in the door and saw what he was doing. Then we knew we were tailing the wrong guy. The paperwork went somewhere else."

"Why would the guy be carrying around this paperwork anyway?"

Felicia shook her head. She'd stopped squinting at me, giving up on getting clear focus. She looked tired.

"It's a long story," she said. "I'll tell you about it later. I've got to get some sleep."

I shrugged, which reminded me that I still had sore muscles in my shoulders.

"I mean, I could understand if you were following some guy because you thought he had cocaine in his briefcase and it turned out he just had paperwork in there. But for it to be the other way around doesn't make sense. What kind of a guy—"

"Bubba."

"Yeah?"

"I've really got to go to bed."

"Okay, sweetie," I said. "You rest well."

I puckered up to give her a good-night smooch, but she couldn't see well enough to pick up her cue and she trudged off to the bedroom smooch-less.

Once alone, I thought some more about Boyd's adultery. I needed to be careful. I couldn't let all the cheaters at The Manor cause me to make a mistake at home. Felicia was working hard. She didn't deserve me suspecting her of stuff she'd never do.

But I still wished she weren't spending so much time with Jake Steele.

Fourteen

Felicia was gone when I awoke Saturday morning. She'd left another note, saying she'd be working much of the day and reminding me of the party at Jake Steele's house that night. Like I needed reminding.

The good news was that I escaped explaining to her how I turned my ankle and broke my camera and got a speeding ticket and generally made an ass of myself. She hears enough stories like that already. The bad news? I still had to tell Nancy Chilton.

I put it off as long as I could. I limped around the house on an ankle that had puffed up and turned purple overnight. I drank coffee and kept my purple foot elevated and read the newspaper and fondly remembered the days when I smoked cigarettes in the morning. I'm glad I quit, but smokers always have something to do during slow moments, such as Saturday mornings when they're putting something off.

I called Melvin Haywood's house a couple of times and left more messages on his machine. I still had trouble believing Turtle Man might've killed Andrew Rollins, but his disappearing act sure wasn't helping matters.

I took a shower, mostly standing on one foot like a pink flamingo, and let the hot water soothe my aching muscles and joints. I shaved and brushed my teeth and got dressed and, except for the limp, looked and felt more like myself.

But on the inside, I was filled with dread. I knew Nancy Chilton would call at some point, asking whether I'd gotten the goods on her husband, and I hated to tell her the truth.

Finally, around eleven o'clock, I couldn't stand it anymore and I dialed her number. A man who sounded very much like Boyd Chilton's TV commercials answered. I swiftly hung up without saying anything. A few minutes later, my phone rang.

"What do you mean, calling here?"

It was Nancy Chilton. She caught me off-guard.

"I, um, well, see—"

"I don't need Boyd getting suspicious," she said, her voice low and angry. "Not until I'm ready to file the divorce papers."

"I didn't say anything," I said. "I just hung up when he answered. How would that make him suspicious?"

She harrumphed. "We've got caller ID, Bubba. If Boyd hadn't been too hung over to care, he might've checked it out and seen it was you."

"I take it he's not there now?"

"He just left. He always goes to the office for a few hours on Saturdays. So now's our chance. Tell me about last night."

"It didn't go so well," I confessed. "Hate to tell you this, but Boyd really is having sex with a young woman. I saw them."

"I knew it!" She sounded triumphant. "And you got pictures?"

"Yes. I mean, no. I had them, but then I lost them."

"What?"

So I explained it all. No way to make myself look hero-

ic. No way to mitigate the damage. I tried to adopt an attitude of world-weariness, a tone that suggested "this kind of
thing happens all the time in the private eye biz." She was-
n't buying it.

"Do you realize what you've done?"

I realized a lot of things, but I owed it to her to play
along. "What?"

"You've tipped him off! Now he knows someone's
watching him. And he'll know I'm behind it. That's why he
was so frosty this morning. I thought he was just feeling
guilty. But he's onto me."

"Not necessarily. There could've been a lot of reasons
someone was taking pictures—"

"Name one."

Okay, she had me there. I couldn't come up with anything. It didn't matter anyway. Her mouth was a runaway
train.

"I can't believe this. I wanted this done on the sly. Boyd's
probably at the office now, shipping his money off to the
Caymans so my lawyers can't get at it."

"Maybe he won't—"

"You've put him on guard, Bubba. That was a terrible
mistake."

I sputtered and consoled and apologized. And then she
surprised me again.

"What do we do now?"

We? I'd figured I was fired. That there was no longer a
"we."

"You want me to stay after him?"

"Well, I should get something for my money, shouldn't
I? So far, all you've done is make the situation worse."

"Yes, ma'am."

"Maybe he's too arrogant to think he's been caught. He got the film. Maybe he thinks he can be careful for a while, and it'll blow over."

I doubted that. If I'd been in Boyd's position, I would've gone back into that apartment and pulled on my pants and told the young woman I'd never see her again. A wily businessman like him should've seen immediately that he was playing with fire, that his wife was hot on his cheating trail. But men have been known to do some stupid things when it comes to sex. Maybe Boyd would make a mistake.

"You're willing to give me another chance?" I asked.

"I suppose so. The damage has been done. There's no way to undo it. But maybe next time you can actually get the evidence."

"I sure can try."

"That's very convincing, Bubba, very reassuring. I hope you can do better than 'try.'"

"Yes, ma'am."

"Here's what we'll do: I'll call you next time Boyd says he has to work late. It might take a while, but I bet he'll go running back to that girl. Then you can catch him in the act. How does that sound?"

What could I say? It sounded like a huge waste of time. I didn't think Boyd Chilton would allow himself to be caught twice. Or, at minimum, he'd learned his lesson about closing the blinds. But I agreed to stay on the case. I needed the money. And I needed a chance to redeem myself.

But after I hung up the phone, here's the phrase that ran through my head: Once burned, twice stupid.

Fifteen

I was on the phone, talking to Melvin Haywood's answering machine, when I heard an ominous rumble outside. Sounded like the throaty gurgling of a Peterbilt's exhaust as it idled at the curb. On our quiet street, that noise usually meant one thing: My father had come to call.

If there was one wild card I didn't need right now, it was Dub. My old man is loud and cranky and profane and sloppy and hard-of-hearing. He's the kind of redneck that people like to call a "character." As in: "That Dub, he's a character. Didja hear about the time he put that live rooster in Mac O'Grady's sleeper cab?"

Dub relishes his curmudgeonly role, hacking and spitting and cursing his way across the country in his semi. He sees himself as a knight errant of the interstate, so every trip—even to the store for beer—is infused with excitement and adventure, at least in his mind. The man has a million stories to tell and he won't stop talking, even if you threaten him with a gun.

Dub's also way too interested in my work as a private eye. He got mixed up in one of my cases a few months ago—don't look at me, it wasn't my idea—and since then he's always meddling in my business. He vanished from my life when I was nine years old, only to reappear nearly thirty years later, just in time to screw up one of my investigations. He seems determined to catch up on all those lost years, all those lessons he never got around to teaching me, by talking, talking, talking to me until one or the other of us dies.

I hung up the phone and leaped to my feet, forgetting for a moment about my tender ankle. I gasped and nearly fell over. Then I hobbled to the front window and peered out between the curtains.

Dub it was. Climbing down from his big rig, which was parked across the street. He's a stringy old man, kind of thick through the middle. Getting out of the shiny black truck with its chrome smokestacks, he looked like a fly climbing out of the ear of a dragon.

I considered whether to hide, pretend nobody's home. I hadn't seen Dub in a couple of weeks—he stops by when his work takes him through town—but I didn't need another all-day jaw about his harrowing experiences on the Open Road.

Dub didn't come straight toward the door, so I had a moment to pick a hiding place. As I watched through the curtains, he strolled around to the far side of the cab. The light shifted behind the tinted windows as the passenger door opened. Oh, boy. If Dub brought one of his truck-driver friends with him, my whole Saturday was gone. They'd spend the day in my kitchen, knocking back longnecks and telling windy tales, and no amount of clearing my throat and looking at my watch would make them move it along.

I was easing the curtains closed when Dub reappeared around the front of the truck. He was grinning. My mother, Eloise Cutwaller Mabry, was on his arm.

I picked my jaw up off the floor and went to open the

door. I might've entertained notions about hiding from my contrary old man, letting him pass through Albuquerque without seeing me this time around. But a man can't keep the door shut when his mother comes to call.

For most folks, the arrival of the parents probably is a homey scene, one reminiscent of happy holidays and kitchen aromas. But I still can't get used to the idea that mine are back together after all those years apart. For them to suddenly appear in my yard together was strange. It was like looking out the window and finding a flock of flamingos or a pyramid of hamburger. Not altogether unpleasant, but surprising and unsettling.

You need a little history here. When I was a kid, we lived in a white clapboard house in the piney woods outside Nazareth, Mississippi. Dub was on the road most of the time, and Mama and I spent a lot of hours together, exploring the forests and hanging up laundry and wringing the necks of chickens.

Then Jesus Christ wrecked our happy home. He appeared one night to Mama in her kitchen, talking in broken parables and eating all our leftover peach cobbler. He had long hair and a beard and a strange light behind his eyes, and Mama never doubted for a minute that he was Our Lord and Savior. Problem was, everyone else in the world believed her Jesus was a drug-addled hippie who'd somehow ended up camped in a wigwam in our woods. The sheriff even arrested him and hauled him in as a fraud. But a judge rolled away the stone—freeing Jesus on his own recognizance—and the hippie vanished before anybody could prove to Mama he wasn't the real deal.

She couldn't just sit home and hug her Bible and revel in the personal attention of Jesus Christ. She had to tell everybody, including tabloid reporters and hair-sprayed TV types, and we became the laughingstock of Mississippi. Small wonder that Dub hit the road one day and never came back.

Something about getting reunited with me moved Dub to also search out Mama at the old homestead a few months ago. I knew they'd been seeing each other again. Dub gave me twinkly-eyed reports on her every time he passed through Albuquerque.

But here they were in the flesh, approaching my porch. Mama's hair was whiter than when I'd seen her last, but she was still thin as an ascetic and she still wore the slightly befuddled expression of a generally happy person who smells something bad.

She was dressed differently, though, and it showed Dub's renewed influence. She wore Wrangler jeans and cowgirl boots and a white sweatshirt with some kind of spangled bird on the front. My mother had always worn loose dresses, faded and worn as feed sacks. To see her dolled up like Queen of the Truck Stop was something of a shock.

I opened the door and Mama released her grip on Dub and ran up the steps toward me, her arms outstretched and her smiling mouth emitting a sound akin to an ambulance siren. I nearly fell over backward before I realized she was just glad to see me. I braced myself for a body-slam of a hug.

She squeezed my shoulders hard—which hurt—and patted me on the back—ditto—and she kissed my cheek. The high-pitched squeal formed into words: "ohlookat you—sogoodtoseeyou—howhaveyoubeen—whatin heavensnamehaveyoubeenupto—isyourwifehere— I'msohappytobehere—haveyouputonweight?"

Past her shoulder I could see Dub rocking on his heels, grinning like a new papa. I felt like pinching him.

Mama leaned back in my aching arms and looked up at my face. She was absolutely glowing.

And I said, "Who are you and what have you done with my Mama?"

She looked confused for a second, but then her smile returned and she said, "Oh, you silly galoot," and she hugged me up some more.

I've visited Mama only a handful of times since I moved out West, but she always was just the same as I remembered from my Mississippi youth. She alternated between wistful and fervent, her whole life revolving around the visitations which had run Dub off. Pining for her Other Man. Jesus.

This keening, spangly woman, clinging to me like a peach on a pit, was way too happy to be my mother.

And that made me look at Dub again. His Groucho eyebrows were bobbing as he leered lasciviously at my Mama's narrow backside. I nearly fell off my sore ankle.

Nobody likes to admit their parents have sex. I'm sorry, but it's just icky. And when the parents have been reunited after a long layoff and they're in their sixties, for Chrissakes, and ought to know better than to get mixed up with each other even if they are still legally married . . . Well, let's just say I didn't want to think about it.

But they showed all the signs. The glow. The grins. The knowing looks. These people, my parents, by all indications, had recently been doing the nasty. And omigod there's a bed right there in that sleeper cab.

I went stiff all over. Mama finally broke her clench and went to a neutral corner so Dub could come up and shake my mitt and slap me on my sore shoulder.

"How are you, son?"

"Fine. What are you two doing here?"

"Surprisin' you. You seem to have something of a limp there."

"Turned my ankle. So you've come to visit?"

"What the hell else would you call it? What's the matter with you, son?"

"Took a fall. Couple of falls. But I'm okay."

"You look like hell."

"Thanks. This is quite a shock, seeing you two. Mama's never been out here before."

"That's why she's so excited."

Mama took up the ululations again, and I hustled them inside before she started speaking in tongues or something.

As I shut the door on the neighborhood, Dub said, "Some fella help you fall down a couple of times?"

"Long story. So, come in, come in. Welcome to my house, Mama."

I looked around. The living room was the usual shambles. Overflowing ashtrays. Piles of newspapers. Unopened mail spilling off the coffee table. Books and magazines lying face-down everywhere, like birds fallen from the sky.

"Why, it's just lovely! What a lovely place!"

She sashayed around the room, cooing over gimcracks and motel souvenirs, while Dub hitched his britches and stretched his back.

"Your Mama's come out on the road with me," he crowed.

"Just this once," she called from across the room, where she was reading one of Felicia's journalism awards, these wooden plaques with brass inscriptions that we've got hanging all over the house.

Dub winked broadly. "I think I'm gonna talk her into coming with me all the time. We're having a lot of fun."

I just bet they were. Mama was all giggly and Dub was giving her the goggle eyes. No wonder he was holding his back and stretching. How big are the beds in those sleeper cabs anyway?

Boy, I needed to stop thinking like that. I offered coffee and we all marched into the kitchen. I cleared some dirty dishes off the table and started a new pot of java and ordered them to sit. Dub scooted his chair around the table so he could sit closer to Mama.

"It's interesting, traveling around," she said, giving Dub the moony eye. "And I finally get out to Albuquerque!"

She said this last to me, and her voice rose, and I was afraid she was going to start squealing again. I cut in quickly.

"I offered to fly you out here for the wedding, but you won't get on a plane."

"Oh, no. I'll stay on the ground, thank you. Until the Lord calls me home and gives me my heavenly wings. Then I'm going to fly around all the time."

Okay, let's not go there. I jumped up and served the coffee. Mama put three teaspoonfuls of sugar in her cup. I don't see how she stays so skinny. I switched to artificial sweetener years ago and I'm still getting fatter. I said something along these lines, to steer Mama away from Jesus talk, and they laughed politely.

"You look good with some meat on your bones," Mama said. "Too bad you're losing your hair, though."

I got some coffee up my nose.

"You're going to end up just like your daddy," she said.

Dub lifted off his baseball cap, which said "CAT" on the front, to expose his mottled, pointy bald head. Wispy gray hair stuck out around his ears. I winced. This is not a look a man anticipates gladly. Not unless he works for Ringling Brothers.

He slapped his cap back on and cackled. "You know what they say about bald-headed men!"

I wasn't exactly sure what they said about bald men, but I guessed it had something to do with virility and I didn't want to hear that, so I said, "Yep. How long are y'all here in Albuquerque?"

"Just overnight. Got a load of furniture parked over at the truck stop. Taking it to El Lay. Timed it so we could spend the night here, maybe take you and that wife of yours out to dinner."

"That's very nice, but—"

"Your mother's idea. I think that's what decided her into coming along with me. She wanted to visit you and figured she'd let me provide the free transportation."

He laughed and grasped her hand in his steering-wheel-deformed claw and they looked into each other's eyes, just beaming, and I wanted to yark all over the table.

"I don't know if Felicia and I will be able to—"

"Speaking of your wife," Mama said, "where is she? I'm so looking forward to meeting her."

"She's working right now."

"When will she be home? In time for dinner at a fancy restaurant?"

She squeezed Dub's hand. All I could think: My God, my parents want Felicia and me to double-date with them.

"I don't know when she'll be home, but we have this thing tonight—"

"You don't know?" Dub blurted. "She didn't tell you when she'd be home?"

"She left me a note—"

"A note! Don't y'all live here in the same house?"

"We've both been working a lot of long hours—"

"That how you got all bunged up? Your ankle and all? Working?"

"Yeah, but what's that got to do with it? See, Felicia works with this guy—"

"What guy?"

For someone deaf enough to hear only half of what you say, Dub is peculiarly impatient in conversation. He wants you to get to the damned point so you'll finish and he can resume talking.

"Guy named Jake. What different does it make? She's been working a lot of long hours with this guy and he's invited us—"

"Long hours? That don't worry you?"

"What?"

"People who work together. They sometimes spend too much time together, if you get my meaning."

"What the hell—"

"Now, now," Mama said, patting Dub's hand. It seemed to have a calming effect on him. "The girl has to work. That's the way things are today. People just work all the time. These days, couples can't afford to let the wife stay home."

"Especially not when the husband's a private eye," Dub hooted. "Right, son?"

Mama gave him a playful little slap on the hand. I considered a different sort of slap.

"So, anyway," I said tightly, "this guy Jake has invited us to a party tonight. I think we have to go."

Mama's face fell, but she propped it back up and gave a

little shrug. I felt like a heel.

Then, right on cue, Felicia blew through the front door.

Oh, that was a merry scene. More hugging and kissing and shrieking than a Kodak commercial. Felicia and Mama hit it off right away, talking with their heads together, laughing about my many shortcomings. Felicia and Dub already are sweet on each other, though I'll never understand why, and he kept throwing his arm around her and crushing her to his chest.

You get the picture. I'll spare you the details. The upshot came fifteen minutes later, after we'd all worn ourselves out welcoming and gushing and shouting hosannas.

Dub began explaining their plan to wine and dine us. I jumped right in.

"I was telling them when you arrived that we have to go to Jake's party tonight."

Felicia protested that she'd rather spend time with my parents. They said they wouldn't dream of taking us away from this big social event in The Manor. The usual give-and-take, back-and-forth, dance-around diplomacy. I wanted to tip the balance toward Jake's party. It would mean spending less time with my lovebird parents. Besides, I wanted to get a look at this guy Jake.

"We must attend the party," I said. "It's important for Felicia's work."

Felicia held up her hands for silence. When we all obliged, she smiled and pushed up her glasses. Then she looked around the table conspiratorially and said, "I have the answer. We'll take them to the party with us!"

I spilled coffee in my lap.

Sixteen

We took Felicia's little Toyota to the party. It was a tight squeeze for the four of us, but we couldn't all fit in the Ram and I sure as hell didn't want to ride up to Jake Steele's house in a Peterbilt. Felicia drove. I rode shotgun, feeling hot and constricted in my blue blazer and gray slacks and leather dress shoes. My parents cuddled in the back seat. They'd doused themselves in competing colognes that filled the car with a fog of fragrance.

Felicia was all smiles behind the wheel. She wore a long, wraparound, flowered, sarong-type deal. It looked complicated and sexy. She looked good and she knew it. But mostly she was smiling because she'd gotten her way again and my parents were making their debut in The Manor.

My face hurt from pretending to smile.

Mama kept giggling.

I'm sure Dub was grinning, too, but I didn't want to turn around to look. No telling what I might find in the back seat.

Felicia swung the car through the entrance to The Manor and the folks "oohed" from the back seat. My face felt like it would crack.

Now, look, I'm not ashamed of my parents. I'm not ashamed of my roots in Mississippi. I automatically stand

up if somebody plays "Dixie." But I didn't want to walk into
this hoity-toity party with my lovey-dovey parents in tow.
Dub would holler and carry on about the Open Road.
Mama might get started on Jesus. There was every possibil-
ity I would die of embarrassment before the night was over.
Embarrassment is too painful a way to go.

The streets of The Manor were dotted with old-fashioned decorative streetlamps that didn't put out much actual light. Most of the houses were ablaze, though. I guess rich
people don't worry about their utility bills. Haywood's
house was dark and forlorn.

Through the afternoon, Dub had wormed out of me
several annoying details about my case. He saw me looking
and said, "That your client's house?"

"Yes."

"Don't look like nobody's home."

I'm thinking, no shit, Sherlock, but I say, "Nope."

"I think he's on the lam," he said. "I bet he's down in
Mexico somewhere, having a good laugh at your expense."

I distinctly heard the pop of one of my fillings coming
loose. I quietly spat several times.

We zoomed up to a Spanish villa. Glowing paper
lanterns danced from the lower branches of towering cottonwoods. Cars crowded the curbs.

"This must be the place," Felicia said as she swung a
Starsky into a tight parking space at her usual breakneck
speed.

More "oohs" from the back seat. Felicia unbuckled her
seat belt and swiveled around to look at my parents.

"Let's not talk any more about Bubba's case," she said
sweetly. "A lot of people at this party are reporters. You
know how we can be. Every little incident sounds like a

story. Bubba's trying to keep this one quiet until he gets it sorted out."

As Nancy Chilton would say: You could've knocked me over with a feather. Never in all our time together has Felicia admitted she'd look the other way if she thought one of my cases merited newsprint. She's usually pissed because her editors see the conflict of interest and won't let her write about me. I've even suspected that she's tipped other reporters to some of my confidential cases. Now here she was, asking my folks to keep my secrets for me. I could've just kissed her, if my face hadn't been all froze up.

My parents murmured promises to keep mum and we all got out of the car.

Jake Steele's inherited home was a two-story affair with iron balconies and a tiled roof. Windows cut deep into its thick white walls. A red flagstone walkway meandered up to the open front door.

My ankle was fine as long as I didn't put any weight on it whatsoever. I didn't want to hop up to the door on my good foot, so I settled for a dignified, war-injury sort of limp.

"Don't guess you'll be doin' any dancin' tonight," Dub said.

Felicia laughed musically. "Bubba doesn't dance. Didn't you know that?"

"Don't dance?" Dub sounded like Gabby Hayes. "Why do you put up with him then?"

"Good question." She gave me a joshing elbow to the ribs. Which hurt.

Then we were through the door and into a world of noise and swirling colors and fleeting smiles and quick handshakes and painful backslaps. I have no idea what I said

to anybody or who they were or how I must've looked,
limping, my face a rictus of dread. All I know is that I sort
of came to and found myself on the opposite side of the living room gantlet, leaning against a wall with my second
bourbon in my hand.

I credited my sudden recovery to the bourbon and took
another healthy slug. It did seem to help. I could now see
individual faces in the crowd of maybe forty people packed
into the one room. Sure, that's Mama right over there.
Showing that woman the rhinestone cross hanging around
her neck on a chain. And Dub? Where did he go? There he
is. By the bar, naturally. Yakking at those two young women.
They're rolling their eyes. Okay. And Felicia? All the way
across the room, back over by the front door. Talking to a
tall, dark, handsome guy. I'd thought she was right behind
me while I swam through the crowd for the bar, but she'd
never made it past the entryway.

More revelers spilled in through the open door and the
handsome man greeted them and shook hands and steered
them into the melee of the party.

Another slug of bourbon and I deduced that the man
was our host, Jake Steele. He and Felicia talked animatedly
by the door. Steele laughed at something she said and
leaned casually against the carved banister of a staircase that
curved up to the second floor. He seemed to be looking at
her funny, sort of out from under his thick black eyelashes.
I think it's what people call bedroom eyes.

I headed toward them. But I decided to get my bourbon
topped off on the way.

I elbowed my way through yuppies and khaki-clad
reporters to reach the rent-a-bartender, who worked the
bottles in a frenzy. Nothing attracts media types like free

booze, and they were pigs around a trough. The red-haired bartender had a large goblet sitting on the counter for tips. The single dollar of seed money looked lonely in there, so I dropped in a buck of my own and looked around archly at the freeloaders who hadn't bothered to tip. They effortlessly ignored me, but the bartender made mine a double, and I felt smug as I squeezed through the crowd toward Felicia and our host.

I heard Dub crowing about something and dared to glance his way. He gestured with his beer bottle as he told some whopper to the two slinky young ladies. They looked around for an escape. Maybe it was the bourbon, but I didn't mind Dub's antics right now. If I kept my distance, maybe nobody would connect me to the loud old man. He looked all right, too. He'd shaved and changed into fresh clothes and traded in his "CAT" hat for a plain black model. I guessed that was his formal cap, which made me smile.

I passed Mama on the way over to Felicia. She was drinking a Coke and smiling blankly at everyone, as if she didn't disapprove of drinking and flirting and sin in general. She still wore her sweatshirt with the spangly bird on the front, but it seemed sort of festive now that I had a couple of drinks in me. I nodded at her and kept moving.

Two broad steps led up from the living room to the entryway and I navigated them successfully and stepped up to Felicia and Jake Steele.

Jake was about three inches taller than me and he looked trim and tanned and unforgivably cool in his crisp white shirt and brown slacks. His black hair was slicked back with some kind of gunk. He wore loafers with those little tassles on the tongues. No socks. His posture was loose and he seemed comfortable in his own skin. He looked like the kind of guy who knows how to dance.

He and Felicia were deep in conversation, and it took them a second to notice me. I tried to decipher what they were talking about, but it was loud and hot in the room and I felt a bit woozy. I bided my time by taking another slug of bourbon, which naturally went down the wrong pipe and caused me to strangle and cough and spray a fine mist onto Jake's shirt.

He took a step back and calmly waited for me to finish spewing.

"Jake," Felicia said over my hacking, "this is my husband, Bubba Mabry. As you can see, he always knows how to make an entrance."

I wiped my hand on my jacket before I shook his. He had a grip like the jaws of a shark, but I managed to pull free before any bones snapped.

"Nice to meet you," he said, his voice deep and resonant. A TV voice. "Felicia's told me a lot about you."

"Really?"

"Not much else to do but talk when you're sitting all night in a company sedan."

I know there's plenty two people can do in a dark car. I've done some of those things myself. In smaller cars. But it comforted me to hear that Felicia had mentioned me. Maybe it was her way of reminding Jake Steele she wasn't available.

"What are you drinking there, Bubba?" Felicia asked.

"Bourbon. Jake here's got a full bar set up for his party."

"How nice. I haven't made it over there yet. I've been keeping Jake company."

Jake gave us a James Bond smile and said something about how he had to be the doorman at his own party.

"I'll get you a drink," I said to Felicia.

"A gin-and-tonic would be nice."

I turned to go fetch her drink, and Jake said, "I'll just have a beer."

I felt a sour look slide across my face, but I nodded brusquely and plunged into the yakking throng again, my sore ankle twinging with every step.

I couldn't carry three drinks at once, so I downed mine while I waited for the bartender's attention. I was definitely feeling the effects of the liquor. My new friend the bartender filled Felicia's drink to the brim and it sloshed on my hand as I bumped and shimmied my way through the press of journalists.

As I reached the steps, I looked up at Jake and Felicia. They were standing even closer and Jake was giving her his sexiest smile. I felt like pouring his beer on his head.

He didn't even have the decency to put some distance between himself and my wife when I handed them their drinks.

Felicia took a sip and thanked me and essentially told me to run along.

"I'll catch up with you in a minute. I've got to talk to Jake. Work stuff."

Being summarily dismissed didn't make me feel any better, but I propped up my fake smile and gave Jake a curt nod and turned back toward the bar. I tripped going down the steps and fell against the back of a heavyset man who, fortunately, kept his balance. If he'd gone over, the whole crowd might've fallen like dominoes. I apologized and the fat guy glared at me and I slinked away.

I fought my way to the bar, looking for Dub, but the two girls he'd been entertaining were listening to some other clown now. To Dub's credit, they didn't seem any more interested in the new guy's stories.

I held up a finger and got another bourbon. Put another buck in the goblet. The bartender and I were getting along swimmingly.

I couldn't find my parents in the crowd, and that worried me a little. I hoped they hadn't slipped off to a bedroom or something.

I stood on tiptoe—which made my ankle stab with pain—to peer over the crowd at Felicia and Jake. Their heads practically touched as they whispered together. Work stuff. They were together all the goddamned time. Why did they need to talk about work now?

Nothing I could do about it, not without making a scene. I drank some more, smiling at semi-familiar faces I'd seen at other office parties. But I didn't engage anyone in conversation. I was too busy fretting.

A hint of evening breeze came through open French doors behind me, and the notion of fresh air drew me like a magnet. The doors opened onto a flagstone patio surrounded by manicured flower beds. A long buffet table was buried under finger food in the center of the patio. Folding chairs ringed it, but only a few were being used. Most of the crowd wanted to stay close to the bar.

My parents were in two of the chairs and Dub had settled into a rapid-fire nosh. His paper plate barely supported all the canapés and finger sandwiches and guacamole he'd piled on it. Mama had a few baby carrots and a single tiny sandwich on her plate, and she picked at them delicately. On either side of them were reporter types, two young guys with bad haircuts and threadbare clothes. They smirked as I spoke to my parents.

"Everything okay?"

"Get yourself something to eat, boy," Dub brayed.

"I'm not hungry."

"So you're with these two?" one of the reporter boys asked. He had a thin beard that barely covered a narrow jaw.

"With us?" Dub exclaimed. "Why, this boy's the fruit of our loins!"

He waggled his brows at Mama, who blushed. The reporters showed toothy grins.

"Dub here was just telling us about the life of a truck driver," the beard said.

I'll bet he was. And I'll bet these two were egging him on. Some journalists, particularly the young ones, are so busy acting jaded about everything in the world, they can't pass up an opportunity to make fun of regular folks and their humdrum lives.

"Dub's full of stories," I said.

"He's full of something all right," Mr. Skinny Beard said, looking sidelong at his colleague.

I felt like punching him, but Dub har-harred. Hell, if it didn't bother my old man to be the butt of ridicule, why should I let it get me riled? I turned to Mama instead.

"You doing okay?"

"Fine and dandy," she said. "I just can't get over what a wonderful house this is. Why, it's just lovely!"

She'd said the same thing about the dump where I live.

"Do you need anything?" I asked her.

"Nope, doing just fine. Your father's looking after me."

"That's right! Got her fed and watered. Ready to put her in the barn for the night!"

Mama twittered. The two slimeballs snickered. I glared at the bearded one until our eyes met.

"I'll be back," I said, hoping for an ominous Schwarzenegger tone.

He snickered some more. Asshole.

I snatched up a finger sandwich and plunged it into my mouth as I headed back inside. Pimento and cheese. Phew. I couldn't spit it into the shrubbery, not with so many people around, so I swallowed it and hurried to the bar. Bourbon, I've found, makes a pretty good mouthwash.

After I'd sucked down half my drink, I looked around for Felicia. She was no longer with Jake, who remained by the door, chatting with a couple of swells. I finally spotted her in conversation with three women over in one corner. The women looked hard-bitten, like they were newspaper types, too, and I didn't want to brave that group. Instead, I saw a chance to get Jake Steele alone.

I wrestled my way through the herd of revelers, who were getting merrier by the minute, thanks to the red-haired bartender. I saw the fat man up ahead and veered right to give him a wide berth. By the time I reached the steps, the couple who'd been talking to Jake had moved on and I had him all to myself.

"Ah, Bubba," he said as I approached, "are you having a good time?"

"Terrific," I said flatly. "But I was hoping to talk to you for a minute. In private."

He cocked a handsome eyebrow, then looked about us.

"Don't think anyone can hear us up here," he boomed over the crowd noise. "What's on your mind?"

I glanced around, but nobody seemed to be paying us the least attention.

"Felicia probably told you I'm a private investigator."

Jake nodded. "Everybody knows that. You're famous

down at the newsroom."

That threw me. "I am?"

"Sure. Everybody knows about that book you wrote with Felicia, where you claimed to have met the living Elvis."

I flinched. That damned book is going to haunt me forever. How come everybody knew about the book when its sales had been so poor? Did they all pass around the same tattered copy? Had they underlined the parts that made me look particularly stupid?

"I don't want to talk about Elvis," I said, "but I do have some questions for you."

Now both of his eyebrows arched. He seemed to have total control over all his features, like an actor or somebody who spent an inordinate amount of time in front of a mirror. I reminded myself that he used to be on television news. Watching himself on the monitors every night, whipping out the somber looks or wry smiles on cue, bathing in makeup and hairspray. Yeech.

"What kind of questions?" he asked.

"About The Manor. Have you lived here long?"

"I grew up here. This house was one of the first ones built in the neighborhood."

He patted the plaster wall nearest him, as if it were a friendly old mare.

"I only moved back recently, after my parents got killed in a car wreck."

I suppose I should've expressed sympathy for his loss, but between the bourbon and my eagerness to ask my questions, I skipped all that and got to the point.

"How well do you know your neighbors?"

He shrugged elegantly. "As well as most people, I suppose. Actually, I know the long-time residents better than some of the newer ones. When I was a teenager, I had a little business, cleaning swimming pools. I used to do most of the pools in the area, so I met a lot of the people here, especially the wives who were home during the day."

I gave him the hard eye. Was he intimating something about lonely housewives? Did it somehow have something to do with Felicia? I felt punchy, as if everyone at this party was making fun of me and my parents and my investigation business. My emotions were unstable. I blamed the bourbon. But that didn't keep me from draining my glass.

Steele still was talking, explaining how he'd left his pool business behind when he went off to college back East.

"You know Andrew Rollins?" I asked.

"Sure. Or, I did. Guess I won't be seeing him around The Manor anymore. Are you investigating his death?"

"Sort of—"

"Isn't that police business? A homicide?"

"Well, yeah, but I have this client—"

"Your client involved in the murder?"

Then I caught myself. What the hell was I doing? This guy, for all his movie star looks, was just another reporter. Sure, it was a social occasion, but anything I said to him could still end up on the front page. Felicia had warned my parents not to talk about my case, and here I was doing it myself.

"It's not about the murder," I said. "Goes further back than that. Did you ever know of Rollins having affairs with housewives in The Manor?"

Jake Steele narrowed his eyes at me and coughed into his fist.

"I wouldn't know about that," he said. "And even if I

did, I wouldn't tell you. Glass houses and all that."

I looked him over. I could imagine him a dozen years earlier, a high school stud with a deep tan and a sparkle in his eyes. I'd bet plenty of The Manor's women had used him to service more than their pools.

"Any of your neighbors here?" I asked, gesturing toward the milling crowd.

"A few. Most of them are people from the *Gazette*."

"Maybe if you could point out one or two neighbors—"

"I don't think so, Bubba. I don't want you grilling my guests. Particularly given the nature of the questions."

I nodded, which made me a little dizzy. I shifted the weight off my bad ankle while I tried to think of some way to knock down his stonewall.

"Are you all right?" he asked genially. "Have you maybe had too much to drink?"

I looked in my glass, which was empty except for melting ice cubes.

"Not yet," I said.

Seventeen

By the time we left the party, I was drunker than a two-peckered hoot owl. I guess it showed because it was very quiet in the car as we drove home. The only sound was Felicia grinding the gears and the occasional stifled burp from Dub. It was an awkward silence, the type that usually follows when somebody makes a scene.

Felicia seemed steamed at me. Had I said or done something untoward at Steele's? I had a little trouble remembering exactly what happened after my conversation with the host.

I know I had a couple more drinks. At least a couple. Bourbon seemed the only remedy for my aches and pains and Felicia's cynical office mates.

I remembered having terse conversations with a few guests. I remembered growling at the reporter with the thin beard some more, enough that he finally slunk away and stopped ribbing my old man.

And I guess I had something to eat because I seemed to be wearing cheese dip on the front of my shirt.

But mostly the evening was a blur of uneasiness. Maybe, in all my attempts to avoid embarrassment, I'd somehow embarrassed Felicia. If so, I'd hear about it soon enough.

"So," I ventured, "did everyone have a good time?"

That lit a fuse under Dub and Mama. They exploded into chatter. Mama praised the house and the food and the guests, who "seemed so nice." Dub proclaimed it the best party he'd ever attended, even though there'd been no fist-fights or dancing girls.

Felicia said nothing. I tried to study her in the light from the dashboard, but my eyes didn't seem to focus very well. I could make out, however, that her jaw seemed to be locked in a jutting position. Not a good sign.

I couldn't just leave it alone, naturally.

"Hon? Did you have a good time?"

She kept her eyes on the road. She spoke, but didn't seem to be moving her lips.

"It was all right," she said. "I'm just tired. I haven't gotten much sleep lately."

I patted her on the shoulder.

"You certainly seemed to have fun," she said through clenched teeth.

I yanked my hand back as if scalded. I needed to ask her what she meant, what I'd done. But I sure as hell didn't want to have such a discussion with Dub and Mama listening from the back seat.

Finally, I volunteered, "Guess I had a little too much to drink."

"You think so?" It wasn't really a question, so I didn't answer. If Felicia had more to say about my drunkenness, it would spew forth eventually. I just hoped she'd wait until we got rid of my parents. Then she could tell me exactly how I'd made a jackass out of myself, vengefully swilling Jake Steele's free booze.

Mama, I suppose, could sense the tension. She sat quietly. Dub was oblivious, as usual.

"Thought you were working that party," he said. "You ask folks about your client and that murder?"

I cleared my throat. We were on I-40 now, circling toward home, and light poles and road signs rocketed past my window. The motion made me queasy.

"I asked a few questions," I said, "but I didn't get anywhere."

I risked a glance at Felicia. Maybe that's why she was mad. Maybe that rat Jake Steele told her I questioned him. She stared straight ahead, her jaw like the tip of an iceberg.

Dub cackled. "Maybe if you hadn't gotten all liquored up, you coulda learned something."

I swiveled my head around to glare at him, which only made me dizzier. I couldn't focus on him in the dark back seat, but I could see his bright Cheshire-cat dentures grinning at me. I faced forward again.

The motion of the little car wasn't sitting well with my inebriation. Just hold on, I told myself, sit quietly until you get home to the comforts of familiar surroundings and Alka-Seltzer and a porcelain receptacle.

Dub insisted on talking. "You've been in some fixes in the past, but I bet this is the first time you've ever worked for a murderer."

I sighed heavily, glanced at Felicia. She never took her eyes off the road.

"There's no proof Melvin Haywood is the murderer," I said.

"Maybe not, but it sure as hell looks suspicious, him disappearing like that."

What could I say? Dub had this ability, amid all his blather, to hit the nail on the head. Though I guess it's a matter of probabilities. If you talk all the goddamned time, once in a while you're going to make sense.

I simply nodded, which caused a sloshing sensation in my head. I closed my eyes and my mouth and sat very still the rest of the way home.

When we arrived, Dub and Mama said their good-nights in the front yard in the light from the porch. Felicia invited them to come in, even asked them to spend the night, which cost me a momentary panic, but the old folks had a motel room near the truck stop and they seemed eager to get there. I didn't want to think about that.

Mama hugged me and I managed not to tip over. Dub pumped my hand and worked his eyebrows and pledged to call from the road in a day or two. While he was gabbing at me, I watched past his shoulder. Mama and Felicia embraced and Mama thanked her for showing them such a good time.

"I'm so glad we finally met," Mama said. "You're quite a young lady. I think Bubba's done well for himself."

Felicia blushed and smiled and some of the ice left her face. I took a chance and sidled over to her and snaked an arm around her shoulders. She went stiff at my touch, but I couldn't jump back, not with my parents watching.

So we stood there, the happy couple, waving as the Peterbilt rumbled away. Then Felicia broke away from me and stalked into the house.

It's four steps up from the yard to our front porch and every one made my ankle hurt. I went up them like a geezer, putting both feet on each step, hanging onto the handrail for dear life. Between my drunkenness and my injuries, I felt lucky to make it into the house without falling.

Felicia hadn't turned on the living room lights and I

couldn't see her anywhere. The idea that she lurked some-where in the dark made me nervous. When Felicia's mad, she tends to come at you quick and fierce. I didn't need her pouncing from darkness.

I found a lamp, nearly knocked it off the table, then got it turned on. No sign of Felicia. I heard water running in the kitchen, so I veered the other direction, down the hall to the bathroom. I locked the door behind me and took sev-eral deep breaths. Safe at last.

Don't get the impression that I'm afraid of my own wife. I mean, she can be a little intimidating. That's one reason she's such a good reporter. But mostly I'm just nervous about any kind of conflict. I still have that newlywed dis-ease, where I'm constantly taking her temperature, asking her if she's happy and so on. I guess I still can't quite believe she settled on a boob like me. I worry sometimes that if I piss her off enough with my fumbling around, she'll get fed up and go find herself somebody else. And that's part of the reason handsome, attentive Jake Steele gave me the trembles. Jake had all the things I don't have—money, looks, charm. If he zeroed in on Felicia, I wouldn't stand a chance.

I braved a look in the mirror and winced. A little green around the gills. My hair had been blown around so that it resembled a tumbleweed. My eyes were glassy and I had something black stuck between my front teeth.

Just the image I wanted Mama to take away with her after seeing me for the first time in years. And just the sort of look that would make a wife wonder why she ever took her husband to office parties.

My stomach gurgled and I tasted bile. Oh, shit. I stripped off my blazer and hung it on a hook on the door. I grabbed a towel off the rack. And then I was on my aching knees, hanging over the toilet, throwing up my own toenails.

Let's just say I was there a long time. And that when I finally, sheepishly, emerged from the bathroom, I expected Felicia to lecture me long and hard on my alcohol consumption.

But there was no lecture. Felicia already was in bed, sound asleep. Somehow, that made me feel worse. I would've preferred the lecture. At least I might've squeezed a little sympathy out of her by acting contrite. For her to just go to sleep when I was in such distress seemed to indicate a certain chilly disregard.

I shucked my clothes and teetered into bed beside her. She didn't stir.

What was wrong with me? I'd dodged a bullet when she went to sleep without laying into me first. Why did I have the urge to shake her awake, to make her tell me all the things I'd done wrong at the party? Was I that desperate to stay in her good graces?

Love can make you crazy. Waking Felicia when she was already angry would've been insane. Better to let her get some rest. Maybe a good night's sleep would defuse the situation.

The bourbon sickness had left me woozy, but wide awake. I lay on my back, my hands behind my throbbing head, staring up at a slowly spinning ceiling. Why had I gotten so shit-faced? I'd been in pain and the bourbon had seemed to help at first. Now, I had all the aches and pains, plus a sick stomach and a pounding headache. As a remedy, bourbon seemed to have some drawbacks.

The main reason I'd poured it down was because smug Jake Steele clearly was flirting with my wife. I couldn't punch him out at his own party, so I'd taken my revenge on his liquor bill. Which was stupid. Jake probably was sitting at home, smiling about Felicia's idiot husband. I, on the other hand, felt as if I'd let Dub drive his Peterbilt over me several times. Who was the loser here?

But, like I said, love will make you do crazy things. And jealousy is love's ugly sister. I'd embraced them both tonight, before I embraced the toilet, and it had cost me.

As I finally closed my eyes, I recognized that I'd gotten a taste tonight of what Melvin Haywood must've felt when he found out his wife had cheated on him. Anger and resentment and lunacy. There was a good chance it had driven him to commit murder.

I told myself I'd never let my emotions carry me that far. I'd get myself under control before jealousy ruined me, before I did something else stupid, like taking a swing at that leering Jake Steele. So far, the only person I'd really hurt had been myself.

Eighteen

I woke late Sunday morning, feeling as if a troop of Nazis had goose-stepped through my head in dirty boots. I wanted to turn over and go back to sleep for, say, a month, and give my body time to recover from alcohol poisoning. But my bladder was having none of that. I had to get up.

Felicia had left me a note by the coffeemaker. Its entire contents: "I'm at the office."

Whew. Clearly, a night's sleep hadn't calmed her down. I told myself I'd call her, try to make nice. If she was ready to unload on me, it would be easier to take over the phone. But first I needed aspirin. And coffee. And an ice pack.

I was on the sofa, working on my second cup of joe, a bag of frozen peas pressed to the back of my neck, when the phone jangled. I didn't want to answer, but I couldn't just let it ring. The bell made my head hurt.

"Hello?"

"Bubba? Hi there. It's Melvin Haywood."

My reply was something like, "Gaaah."

"You've been trying to reach me?" he asked. "I called my house to check my messages and there were about a hundred from you."

He didn't sound like a man on the run. His voice sounded light, sort of breezy. If he'd killed Andrew Rollins, he wasn't feeling a great deal of remorse.

"Where are you?" I croaked.

"Right now, I'm sitting on a beach, talking on a cell phone. I've got a drink with a little umbrella in it. Can you believe that?"

It was hard to picture the turtle washed ashore. I'd expected Melvin Haywood to be sweating behind the wheel of a car on some remote desert highway, checking his mirrors for the dreaded flashing lights.

"The police are looking all over for you!" I blurted.

"The police?"

"You're wanted for questioning."

"My God. Questioning about what?"

Pain stabbed my temples. If Haywood was faking it, he was pretty convincing. If he wasn't faking, then he didn't know about Rollins' murder. Which meant I got to tell him about it. I didn't feel up to it. I took a deep breath, but the air tasted sour.

"The death of Andrew Rollins."

"What? Rollins is dead?"

"Murdered."

"Oh my Lord. What happened?"

"Somebody clubbed him with a dumbbell at his clinic."

"At his clinic? That doesn't make any sense. Why would—"

"The police think you did it."

"What?"

"They, um, wanted to know why I was nosing around the clinic. I had to tell them about you."

Haywood sputtered into the phone. There was a crash and then silence.

I said "hello" a couple of times, but there was no

answer. I waited.

"Bubba? Are you still there?"

"Yeah. What happened?"

"I literally fell out of my chair. Spilled my drink all over." Then his voice dropped to a near-whisper. "I can't believe the police are hunting me."

"'Hunting' may be too strong a word. They want to ask where you were when it happened, stuff like that. Nobody knew where you've been the last few days."

"I took a vacation. The first one in years. The first one— ever—by myself. It's been a year since Eileen's cancer diagnosis. I thought I should go off somewhere and think about that turning point in my life. But now to find out I'm wanted by the police—"

"Just for questioning."

"And you told them about me?"

"I had no choice. They suspected me. I had to explain why I was so interested in Rollins."

"You told them about him and Eileen?"

"I couldn't help it—"

"Oh, Bubba. I wish you hadn't done that. If word gets out that she had an affair—"

"Your wife's reputation is the least of your problems right now. You need to get back here and talk to the cops. The longer you're gone, the worse it looks."

Silence.

"Mr. Haywood?"

"I'm thinking."

"There's not much to think about. If you don't come in for questioning—"

He didn't let me finish. "When was Rollins killed?"

"Thursday morning."

"What time?"

"I don't know exactly. Early. Around eight, I guess."

"Oh, my."

"What?"

"I flew out Thursday morning, but my plane didn't take off until ten."

"Where were you at eight?"

"At home. Packing."

"Can anyone vouch for that?"

"That's the problem. I practically sneaked out of town. I thought, if I went by the office, if I saw anyone I knew, I'd talk myself out of this irresponsible trip. That's what always happened in the past. I needed to get away. I needed to sort things out."

"I understand. But the cops could say you killed Rollins, then went straight to the airport and skipped town."

More silence.

"I didn't do it, Bubba. You have to believe that. I couldn't kill anybody."

What to say? Comfort him? Suggest a plan of action? Should I even believe him? Maybe he had bopped Rollins and then split. He'd obsessed about Eileen's infidelity for months. Was he jealous enough to kill her lover? I couldn't imagine my gray little client swinging a dumbbell at Rollins' head. But it looked bad and I told him so.

"Then we have a problem to solve," he said matter-of-factly, as if a murder investigation was just another audit to face. "You've got to help me, Bubba."

Help him? It was my fault we were in this mess. How could I help him? How could I even think about a solution while my hangover did a twenty-one-gun salute inside my head?

"You want to hire me?" I asked, trying to keep the incredulity out of my voice.

His voice dropped an octave. "I've already hired you. I believe you're still on retainer."

"Yeah, but—"

"And to tell the truth, I haven't gotten much for my money so far."

"I found out about Rollins—"

"And then told the police all about it! How could you do that?"

I stammered.

"Now you can help me prove I didn't kill him."

"But I—"

"Come on, Bubba. You're my only hope. I can't prove my innocence from here."

I started to ask him where "here" was, then thought better of it. Romero would worm it out of me, first chance he got. Better not to know. I told Haywood so before he could say more.

"But how will you reach me? I need to know what's going on back there."

"Check your messages every day. I'll nose around, see what I can find out. I'll let you know when the coast is clear."

"Should I just come back there? Talk to the police? Maybe I could persuade them—"

"No, don't do that. Not yet. You've already been missing for four days. Another day or two won't matter. I can talk to the cops, maybe figure a way out of this."

"I'm supposed to fly back to Albuquerque on Wednesday."

"Maybe I'll make some progress before then."

We both said nothing for a while. Only the hiss of static on the line to interrupt our thoughts.

"There's really only one answer," he said finally.

"Yeah, what's that?"

"You've got to find the real killer."

My stomach flopped. "I'll see what I can do."

Then Haywood said good-bye. I hung up and let my head fall back against the sofa.

Find the killer. Right now, I felt so bad I couldn't find my own ass.

Nineteen

I was flat on my back on the couch when Felicia got home three hours later. I was still in my bathrobe. I still felt like warmed-over shit. And I still didn't have the slightest idea how to get Melvin Haywood off the hook.

Felicia stopped just inside the living room door. She wore jeans and a loose white blouse and sneakers and her hair was damp from the heat outside. She gave me the once-over, her hands on her hips.

"You look like hell," she pronounced.

"People keep telling me that."

"Hung over?"

"And then some."

She shook her head. I still hadn't worked out a good way to apologize for my behavior at Jake Steele's party. It would've helped if I had a better idea of what I'd done wrong, other than swimming in bourbon. It's hard to make excuses when you don't know your sins. Now that Felicia finally was home, I figured she'd fill in the blanks.

I struggled to a sitting position, better for confession and contrition.

"Guess I made an ass of myself last night."

She cocked her head and grinned at me. A sliver of hope broke on my dark horizon.

"You sure got drunk," she said. "Your Mama was worried about you. She asked me if you always drink like that."

"What did you tell her?"

"I told her no. Sometimes it's worse."

"Thanks. She's probably praying for me right now."

"Looks like you could use it. Have you eaten anything?"

The thought of food made my stomach do the samba. I shook my head.

Felicia sat down beside me. She lit a cigarette and let smoke trail out her nose. She looked like she was breathing fire, and I flinched, still expecting her to unload on me.

"Why did you drink so much?" she asked calmly.

"I don't know. I guess I was uncomfortable, you know, with Dub there carrying on. And your co-workers were making fun of him."

"I understand you let them hear about that," she said.

I said nothing. I wasn't sure exactly what I'd said or done. Better to let her tell me.

"I saw one of them today in the newsroom. Benjamin Dover?"

"Which one was he?"

"Young guy. Skinny. Has kind of a thin beard?"

Uh-oh. Him, I remembered. I nodded cautiously.

"He said you threatened him."

"I did?"

"Something about 'ripping out his lungs.' Do you remember saying that?"

"Not exactly, but it's possible. He was baiting Dub. I couldn't stand it."

"So you were defending Dub's honor?"

"When you put it that way, it sounds stupid. Let's say it was the bourbon talking."

She nodded and pushed up her glasses and took another drag off her cigarette. The smoke smelled dry and hot. Made me even queasier.

"I figured it was something like that," she said. "Dover can be an asshole. At least you didn't take a swing at him."

"I came close. Fortunately, I'm already all beat up. I didn't want to take a chance on him swinging back."

"Still feeling rough, huh?"

"Yeah. The swelling's gone down on my ankle, though. I'm healing. Mostly, I've just got a hangover now."

"I'm not surprised. You really poured it down."

I took a deep breath. Here goes nothing.

"Is that why you were mad at me?"

"Who, me? I wasn't mad."

"After the party, in the car, you were mad. I could tell."

"I wasn't thrilled about the way you got so drunk, but I wasn't angry. I had a headache and I just wanted to hurry home and take some aspirin. And I was beat. This project has worn me down. We've been working around the clock. Seeing all those same faces from the office didn't help. I need some time away from those people."

I was so relieved that I wasn't on Felicia's shit list that I wasn't careful enough about what I said next.

"I can see that. They're a pretty snarky bunch."

She gave me the hard eye. "You don't like my co-workers?"

"I'm sure they're fine people. But I didn't like the way they teased my parents. And they always treat me like alien scum."

"Oh, they do not."

"Uh-huh. I tried talking to some of them and they just brushed me off."

"You were drunk. You're not easy to talk to when you

get like that."

What was I doing? I'd survived the recap of my drunken behavior at the party. Felicia didn't seem ready to kill me after all. Why was I pushing it now?

"You're right," I said quickly. Those are two words she loves to hear. "I should've known better than to drink so much. I'm paying the price today."

"Why don't you go back to bed?"

"I was waiting for you. I thought we might need to talk."

"About what?"

"Never mind. Bed sounds good. You look like you could use some rest, too."

She shrugged. "Maybe so. Nothing else I can do at the office today. Jake took the day off to clean up after his party. I might as well catch a nap."

"Let's both go."

So we did. Here I was, faced with the challenge of proving my absentee client didn't commit murder, and I was trooping off to bed. I can't justify it. I should've pulled myself together and gone out in search of evidence. There had to be some way to clear Haywood, to give him an alibi that would stand up, but I was in no condition to pursue it.

Felicia may have had something more than a nap on her mind. We've been known to spend Sunday afternoons in bed, practicing our sexual acrobatics. If so, I never found out. I was asleep before my head hit the pillow.

It wasn't a restful sleep. I felt too sick for that. I tossed and turned queasily. Plus, I dreamed the whole time about Felicia and that bastard Jake Steele.

Twenty

I slept all afternoon and through the night, and felt better when I arose early on Monday. I still was stiff all over, but a hot shower helped. My ankle could take my weight, though I wouldn't be running any footraces anytime soon, and my elbow had scabbed over nicely. All in all, I felt ready to face the world again.

By nine o'clock, I was at the cop shop downtown, asking to see Lieutenant Steve Romero. The sergeant at the front desk was a burly white guy with a crewcut and a world-weary expression. He looked at me like I was something that had crawled out from under a rock. I get that a lot, particularly from people in authority, but I didn't let it bother me as he called upstairs to Romero. I took a seat on a scratched-up plastic chair. This guy was just a stepping stone to Romero and I waited quietly, figuring I wouldn't even get my feet wet. Naturally, nothing's ever as easy as it first appears.

The sergeant hung up the phone and gestured me back over to the desk.

"Romero said to ask what you want."

I looked at the phone and back at the grim sergeant. If he had questions from Romero, why had he hung up?

"I need to talk to him about one of his cases," I said.

"What case?"

What case? What the hell did this guy care? Did he even have any idea which cases Romero handled?

"A homicide case," I said.

The sergeant made a face like he'd just stepped in dogshit.

"Of course, it's a homicide case," he said through tight lips. "That's all Romero handles. The lieutenant wants to know which case."

Now, see, I knew something was wrong here. Romero should've known it was the Rollins case. What other homicide had I been involved with lately? Was there some other killing I didn't know about?

The sergeant's questions made me cautious.

"Andrew Rollins?"

The cop's heavy eyebrows rose. "That's the sports doctor who got killed?"

"Right."

"I heard about that. What do you know about it?"

"Shouldn't I be talking to Romero?"

"Talk to me."

"I'd really feel more comfortable talking to him."

"You and Romero are pals, huh?"

"That's right. Are you sure he told you to ask me all these questions?"

"Sure."

I felt my teeth grinding and waggled my jaw, trying to get the muscles to relax.

"Won't he ask me a whole 'nother set of questions when I get up to his office?"

"You'd have to take that up with him."

I ran my fingers through my hair. We were getting

nowhere at the speed of light.

"Could you call him again? Ask him if I could come up?"

"No, I don't think so."

"Why not?"

"Because you can go up now."

The sergeant leaned back in his chair, grinning fiercely.

Muttering, I turned toward the elevator and took a few steps. Then I went back around to the front of the desk.

"When you called Romero, what did he say exactly?"

The sergeant smiled again. It clearly wasn't his customary expression.

"He said to give you a bunch of shit, then let you go on up."

"He did, did he?"

The sergeant nodded.

"And he did this just to improve your mood, right?"

The sergeant grinned again. "I sure feel better. How about you?"

I grumbled some more and went to the elevators.

When I got to Romero's office, he was hanging up the phone. He, too, was smiling, and I guessed the sergeant had called ahead to tell of his success in driving the private eye nuts.

"What's the big idea?"

Romero tried to look innocent, but he couldn't keep the smile off his face.

"Just starting the work week right," he said. "What do you want, Bubba?"

"I heard from Melvin Haywood."

Romero's eyebrows rose and he gestured me into an empty chair. Like I needed any help deciding where to sit.

Every other surface was covered in stacks of paperwork. Sometimes I think he's trying to re-create the Great Wall of China in his small office.

"Where is he?"

"I don't know." I was prepared for that question, and glad I didn't have an answer.

"What?"

"He called me on the phone. He didn't say where he was calling from."

Romero rocked back in his chair and glared at me. "He didn't say, or you didn't ask?"

"Little of both. I figured if I knew where he was, I'd tell you before I was ready."

A smile tugged at the corners of his lips, but he kept it under control.

"You always worm things out of me," I said. "I figured it was better to be ignorant."

Okay, so I fed him a straight line. I expected some crack about my ignorance, but he just sighed and leaned his elbows on the desk.

"Why don't you start at the beginning?"

I gave him a blow-by-blow account of my conversation with Haywood, including his denial of guilt in Rollins' murder.

"How did he sound?" Romero asked when I was done.

"Far away. It wasn't a great connection."

"No, I mean was he convincing?"

"Sure."

"Sounded like he was surprised to hear Rollins was dead?"

"Yeah."

"And you believed him?"

"You'd have to see this guy, Steve. He's not the kind who could kill somebody."

Romero nodded, but his face read, "That's what they all say."

"Really," I insisted. "For Haywood, sneaking off on a quick vacation is like a cardinal sin. He couldn't live with himself if he'd offed the doc."

Romero rocked back in his chair and laced his thick fingers over his chest. "So now you're out to find the real killer, get your client out of trouble?"

"I don't know anything about finding killers. That's your job. But I thought if I told you I'd heard from Haywood, maybe you'd give me a break."

"You want *me* to help you find the killer?"

"I thought we could share information, you know? We've done it before."

"Not when you were representing the number one suspect."

That stumped me for a moment.

"C'mon, Steve. I told you what I know. Shouldn't you share?"

Romero shook his head.

"But I told you—"

"You're doing it again, Bubba. You come to me, begging for help, so you can get paid to do something I'm already doing for the taxpayers. Does that make any sense?"

"No, but it's worked before. Admit it, sometimes you need somebody like me out there, stirring the pot."

"I wouldn't admit that if you were pulling my fingernails out one at a time."

"It's true."

"No, it's not. Look around, Bubba. You're at the police

station. We have rules here. We do things by the book. We don't need some lamebrained private eye messing around in a homicide investigation."

I could see I wasn't getting anywhere. I stood up to leave.

"You can't keep me from nosing around in it," I said as a parting shot.

Romero smiled. I didn't like that.

"No, I can't. But I'll tell you something, Bubba. You get in my way, and I'll press charges against you."

"What charges?"

"How does murder sound?"

"You don't believe I killed Rollins."

"No, but I could put you on ice for a while before a judge throws out the charges. And I could make sure they get your face on the TV news. Think that would help business?"

"You wouldn't do that." My voice had a quaver in it.

"Try me."

He wasn't smiling now. I ducked my head and got the hell out of there.

Twenty One

S o here's how my deductive mind worked: Let's say for a
minute that Melvin Haywood didn't kill Rollins. Say, in
fact, that Rollins' death had nothing to do with the long-
ago affair with Eileen Haywood. Let's say it was a coinci-
dence he got bumped off less than twenty-four hours after
I tell Haywood he's the one. Then where do I look for the
real killer?

First, I needed to know more about Andrew Rollins. I
needed to know why someone other than Haywood would
feel moved to bash in the good doctor's head.

I couldn't learn anything at his clinic, not without risking another flying lesson from Mystery Meat. The same
went for questioning the widow. So I did what any red-
blooded private eye would do when he needed information
about a doctor. I went to the hospital.

I mentioned before how much I hate doctors' offices.
Well, it goes double for hospitals, with their disinfectant
smells and echoing hallways and lurking germs. They give
me the willies. But I knew a surgeon at University Hospital
who might help me out and I braved the sniffling crowd in
the lobby to find him.

The nurse at the front desk looked like she could be the
police sergeant's sister. She asked me a similar number of

stupid questions before I finally persuaded her to page Dr. Wally Hoffman.

I'd handled a case for Hoffman a couple of years back. He'd been in an ugly custody battle over his son, who was six years old at the time. He suspected the kid's mother was going out at night and leaving the boy alone in her apartment. I pulled a stakeout on her place for a few nights and got some fine photographs, not only of her abandoning the boy, but also of her returning around midnight, drunk, with a boyfriend in tow. My work helped Hoffman win custody of Wally Jr. I'd seen in the newspaper that Hoffman had remarried recently, and I was glad Junior ended up in a happy home.

I figured his dad owed me one.

Dr. Hoffman finally showed up in the lobby, wearing loose green scrubs and white Nikes. He was a stubby guy with frizzy black hair and pale skin that showed he hadn't shaved lately. He had dark circles under his eyes.

He apologized for the delay, explaining that he had just finished up in the operating room. I looked him over, searching for blood spatters, but he apparently was a tidy surgeon. He invited me upstairs to a small office he maintained near the ORs.

Once we were settled, him behind a desk and me on a lumpy sofa that looked as if it got a lot of use by sleepy interns, I told him what I was after.

"You probably knew Andrew Rollins, right?"

He studied his fleshy hands, which were pink from constant washings. "I knew him, but I don't know whether I should say anything about him."

"Don't worry, doc. It's just between you and me. I'm trying to get a feel for the guy."

He looked at me from under thick eyebrows. "How do I know you're not wearing a wire?"

Wearing a wire? Apparently, Hoffman was guilty of watching too many cop shows on TV, too.

"What do you want me to do? Take off all my clothes?"

I stood and grasped the hem of my shirt, as if I was about to pull it off over my head.

He waved his hands at me to show it wasn't necessary.

"Sit down, Bubba. Jeez."

"You ought to be able to trust me," I said as I flopped back onto the couch. "I helped you out once."

"I know you did." His voice had a little whine in it. "But doctors make it a point not to bad-mouth each other. And Rollins is dead now—"

"Just give me an inkling. Tell me what you know about him. Introduce me to a few of your colleagues. Let me ask them the same questions. Maybe somebody will say something that will help me figure out who killed him."

He hesitated, then shrugged his round shoulders. "I don't suppose it could hurt anything. It's not like Rollins will care now. Ask away."

"That's better. Okay, was Rollins well-liked around here? He have any enemies?"

Hoffman looked like he was trying not to smile. "Go out in the hallway. Stop anybody who works here. That person would've considered Rollins an enemy."

"Really?"

"He was an asshole, Bubba. His clinic made a lot of money and he always came to the hospital with this attitude, like he was doing us a favor even showing up. He was rude to the nurses. Condescending toward his patients. The worst."

I whistled.

"I only met him once," I said, "and it wasn't under the best of circumstances, but he seemed like a jerk to me, too. Guess he wasn't just putting on act."

Hoffman shook his head. "I never saw him behave any other way."

"What makes a guy act like that?"

"Beats me. I just open up people's bodies and put them back together. I can't ever figure what's going on in their heads."

I mulled that for a moment. Hoffman looked at his wristwatch.

"Lotta egos in this business," he said. "It's like that old joke. How many surgeons does it take to screw in a light-bulb? Just one. He holds the bulb and the whole universe revolves around him."

I cocked my head.

"You get to act like God when you're a surgeon, life or death in your hands. Some people let that go to their heads."

"I can see how it would."

Hoffman pooched out his lips. "Not after you lose a few patients. Try to explain to their families how they died on the table. That'll bring you back to Earth."

I seized on that. Maybe an angry patient or a grieving relative was behind Rollins' murder. I posed the question to Hoffman, but he was shaking his woolly head before I finished asking.

"Highly unlikely. Rollins repaired knees and elbows. Helped fat ladies lose weight. Got people in shape for big games. I doubt if he ever lost a patient."

"Still, somebody could've been disappointed with his performance—"

"Enough to kill over it? I doubt it, Bubba."

I figured Hoffman was right. It's too easy to sue for malpractice these days. Why resort to murder?

He looked at his watch again.

"Listen, this is interesting and all, but I've got another surgery coming up. I'd sure like to stretch out on the sofa for a few minutes first. My feet are killing me."

"Okay, I'll wrap it up," I said. "Just one more question and then maybe you could introduce me to a few people who knew Rollins."

He nodded.

"Here's the question: Rollins was something of a womanizer, right?"

He held up his pink hands in a "who knows?" posture.

"I'd heard rumors," he said. "And he was on, what, his third wife?"

"Yeah. Charisse. A real pistol."

I smiled at my own joke, but Hoffman didn't get it, naturally. He looked impatient.

"Ever hear any other rumors, like maybe he diddled some of his patients?"

"Never. Even someone as arrogant as Rollins wouldn't take a chance like that."

"How do you mean?"

"We're walking targets. Doctors, especially surgeons, get sued all the time. And everything rides on our reputations. Rollins wouldn't have risked his livelihood to get frisky with some tennis player or something. He had too much on the line."

I shrugged. "People make mistakes."

"Not Rollins. Not a mistake of that caliber. The guy was rolling in dough, by all accounts. He wouldn't have any trouble meeting women outside of his practice."

That made sense. But it didn't explain why Rollins had slept with a patient and neighbor named Eileen Haywood.

I thanked Hoffman for his time and he showed me out the door. In the hall, we ran into a couple of other docs, dressed in surgical scrubs, and he introduced me to them and urged them to give me a few minutes.

I questioned them individually and their answers were remarkably similar to Hoffman's. I tried a couple of the OR nurses. They were less forthcoming about Rollins' short-comings—guess they spent their whole lives trying to keep egomaniac surgeons happy—and I didn't learn much from them either.

Finally, I'd had enough of the hospital. I hurried out of the building and gulped fresh air and put a hand to my forehead. I didn't feel feverish or have that yucky sensation of having caught a germ, and I found some relief in that.

But I wasn't any closer to finding Rollins' murderer.

Twenty Two

I didn't really have a plan for what to do next, but the Ram drove itself over to The Manor. I parked on the street outside Rollins' fancy home. His widow could be my best source of information, if I could only get her to talk to me. I told myself she might be more amenable to a chat now that she'd had a few days to recover from the shock of her husband's murder. I got out of the truck and looked around nervously, searching for any sign of Ed Salisbury.

All was quiet, so I summoned up my courage and approached the front door. Before I got there, though, I heard voices coming from behind the house. Giggling. Sounded like Charisse. The deep rumble of a masculine voice. I crept around the house, stepping over flower beds and around shrubs, keeping an eye out for Mystery Meat.

The back yard was well tended, with gnarly cottonwoods hanging heat-limp branches over an emerald lawn. A board fence encircled the pool area and the voices were coming from there. I hid behind the thick trunk of a cottonwood, hoping neighbors weren't calling the cops about a prowler, and tried to listen. I couldn't make out what was being said, but it definitely sounded like Charisse back there with some man.

I tiptoed across the lawn, my head whipping around for

anyone who might sound the alarm. The fence was seven feet high and I couldn't see over it unless I got a ladder. Flowering bushes had been planted along the base of the fence and bark chips surrounded their stems. I didn't want to step in the flower beds for fear of causing a rustle.

The fence made a corner near the house and I slipped over to it, hoping for a gap between the planks. Sure enough, there was a tiny space where the two walls met. I braved a peek.

Charisse lay face-down on a chaise longue beside the pool, not ten feet away from my peephole. She was stark naked and tanned all over. Ed Salisbury sat in a chair beside her, rubbing suntan lotion on her back.

I was so surprised that I nearly yelped. But I caught myself and inhaled slowly and looked again.

Salisbury was facing my general direction. The slightest movement at my gap in the boards might catch his attention. I stood very still. He was wearing a black Speedo that barely covered the subject. With his strong jaw and bulging muscles, he looked like artwork off a Grecian urn. No wonder the women at the clinic were gaga over him.

Ed let his lotion-slick hand slide down Charisse's back and over her firm buttocks. He dipped his hand between her legs and she giggled and wiggled around on the chaise.

Oh, boy. Even a slow-witted detective could see something was going on between these two. And that changed everything, didn't it? If Charisse had been having an affair with her husband's top assistant, didn't they share all kinds of motive for wanting Andrew dead?

Mystery Meat leaned over to nuzzle the back of Charisse's neck. She cooed. I'd had enough. I used the moment to slip away.

I scurried around the house to the Ram and got behind the wheel. Remembering what occurred the last time Salisbury caught me at the Rollins home, I started the engine and drove up the street a few blocks. Once I had the safety of distance, I parked and used my cellular phone to call Steve Romero.

I had to jump through the usual hoops to get past the switchboard and through the cadre of detectives who work in Homicide, but soon I had Romero on the horn.

"Hi, Steve. I've got some information for you."

"What is it now, Bubba?" He sounded cranky. Maybe my news would cheer him up. I dropped my bombshell.

"I've got evidence that Charisse Rollins and Ed Salisbury are having an affair."

I waited for a response. And waited. Finally, Romero said, "Yeah? So?"

"What do you mean, 'so?' Don't you see what that means?"

Romero took a deep breath and huffed it out into my ear. "What does that mean, Bubba?"

"If they're having an affair, doesn't that make Salisbury a suspect? I mean, he's got motive out the ass, doesn't he? Kill his boss, nail the wife, take over the business. Don't you think he and Charisse could've cooked up the murder?"

Silence.

"C'mon, Steve. This is good stuff. You should be excited. I'm over at Rollins' house right now. Charisse and Salisbury are out by the pool, making out. Don't you want to run over here, catch them in the act, ask some questions?"

"No."

"No? What's the matter with you?"

"I already knew about the affair, Bubba."

"What?"

"Within an hour of the death, I'd learned Salisbury and the wife were involved."

"But—"

"And, sure, in normal cases, that would make him a suspect. He's certainly big enough to cream somebody with a dumbbell."

"Then why—"

"He's got an ironclad alibi," Romero said. "When Rollins was killed, Salisbury was in the other exercise room at the clinic, leading a class. The man's got forty eyewitnesses who say he never left the room."

Shit. Romero was way ahead of me. Again. And, as much as I'd like to see Salisbury get in trouble, it sounded like there was no way to pin the murder on him.

"Maybe it was Charisse," I said. "Maybe she slipped in there and did it while Salisbury was in the other room, building his alibi."

"I thought about that, too."

"And?"

"And don't you think someone would've noticed if she was in the building? That pug-ugly nurse who works the front desk? We couldn't find anyone who'd seen Charisse anywhere near the clinic that day."

"Maybe she was in disguise."

"Maybe you're grasping at straws. Look, I've already checked it out. They're clean. It looks suspicious, but we can't put them in the room with Rollins when he was killed."

Damn. I held the phone to my ear, waiting for another salvo from Romero. He didn't disappoint me.

"Your boy Haywood still looks like the killer. Heard from him again?"

"No, but I didn't expect to. Listen, did anyone at the clinic remember seeing him there? I mean, how did he get past the front desk to whack Rollins?"

"I'd like to ask him that question myself. If he ever comes out of hiding."

"He's not in hiding exactly—"

"As you said this morning. But it sure as hell looks wrong, him disappearing the same morning Rollins was killed."

What could I say? He was right, as usual. I was too flummoxed to come up with any other theories, so I turned on Romero instead.

"You know, if you'd shared some of this information with me, I wouldn't have bugged you with this. I mean, if you knew about the affair—"

"Don't start that again, Bubba. I've got a million things to do today. If you get something good, something new, give me a call."

"Why should I feed you information when you won't give me anything in return? This friendship seems like a one-way street to me. Why didn't you— "

"Bye, Bubba."

Twenty Three

Thirty minutes later, I was at my kitchen table, eating a bologna sandwich and some Fritos and having a beer. The food didn't even wait to get to my stomach before it started giving me indigestion.

I should've known better than to call Romero right away. I'd acted on impulse, a persistent problem with me. That, and a genetic gullibility I inherited from Mama. Together, they lead me to jump to conclusions. I should've expected that Romero already had explored the possibility that Rollins' heir and his top assistant had conspired to murder him. They stood to gain the most, after all.

What did Melvin Haywood stand to gain? Not much. Revenge isn't a tangible benefit from an act so rash, though it did make a pretty good motive. Perhaps he simply let his emotions take over for a moment. One swift, reckless motion and Rollins was dead on the floor. Then the regrets. Skipping town. Once safely out of the cops' grasp, it would've been easy for a smart guy like Haywood to cook up his "vacation" tale and feed it to an idiot like me.

But it just didn't fit. Haywood was a turtle. And turtles don't operate on impulse.

I wanted to believe Charisse and Salisbury were behind the killing. Not just to get Haywood off the hook, either.

They were guilty of messing around behind Rollins' back, and I wanted them to take the fall for his death, too.

Was there anybody in The Manor who wasn't committing adultery? Everywhere I turned, people were running around on their spouses.

Now I'm no prude. I've trailed too many wayward spouses to believe all marriages are rosy and sound. But married life had been pretty good to me so far, and I just couldn't understand all these people being led around by their genitals. Couldn't they stick to one lover? Didn't their vows mean anything?

One could argue that Rollins hadn't exactly been Mr. Fidelity himself. He'd dumped two previous wives. He'd likely slept with Eileen Haywood and God only knows how many others. But that didn't give Charisse and Meat the right to kill him. I wanted them to be punished for their sins.

Christ, I was beginning to sound like Mama.

I took another bite from my sandwich and chewed angrily. Sometimes it sickens me, doing my job. How can a person like me, who regularly sees people at their worst, trust anybody? How can I believe in the goodness of humankind when I so often see them stabbing each other in the backs? How did betrayal become the standard currency of human relationships?

I heard Felicia come in the front door. The timing seemed portentous.

"Bubba?" she called from the living room.

"Back here." I didn't get up from the table. I was too chewed-up inside to move around. I wondered whether I should even see her when I was such a bad mood.

She came through the kitchen door. She was wearing a

loose sundress with sandals and no hose. The sunlight streaming in from the living room backlit her and I could see the silhouette of her lean body through the dress. Usually, I would've gawked with pleasure. But today, it only reminded me that other men probably had seen the same thing. Those snarky reporters at the Gazette probably maneuvered around all day, trying to get her between them and the light.

"Hi," I said glumly.

"Didn't wait supper for me?"

I looked at my watch. It was 3:30 in the afternoon. Hardly suppertime. I'd thought I was working on lunch.

"Just a snack," I said. "It's been a long day."

She flopped into a chair across from me and kicked off her sandals.

"Long day for me, too. But Jake and I are almost finished with the project."

Jake. She would have to mention Jake.

"I've been fighting with editors and lawyers all day," she said. "They're all craven, as usual. Afraid going with the facts will land them in a lawsuit."

"Yeah? And how did Jake handle that?"

She looked at me quizzically.

"He didn't. I dealt with them. He's still chasing after car dealers. We've got one more that we've nearly got nailed."

I harrumphed and took another bite of my sandwich. It tasted like sawdust.

Felicia frowned at me. "Something wrong?"

"No, nothing," I said through a mouthful of sawdust. "I just get a little tired of hearing about Jake all the time."

Her face hardened. "Sorry if I'm bothering you, talking about work."

I took another swig of my beer. Now would be a good time to shut up. Better that I chew off my own tongue than say out loud what had been troubling me for days.

"It's not your work that's bugging me," I said, regretting the words as soon as they spilled from my mouth. "It's that asshole Jake. He's got the hots for you."

A rosy glow crept onto her cheeks. Embarrassment? Irritation? Guilt?

"That's just silly," she said finally. "We work together. That's all."

"You spend every waking minute together."

"It's a big project, Bubba. An award-winner. We're going to put people in jail."

I chugged the last of the beer and set the bottle down on the table a little too hard.

"Hasn't he been putting the moves on you?" I asked churlishly. "You two looked pretty cozy together at that party."

Felicia straightened in her chair. Her face had gone even redder.

"Are you suggesting something's going on between Jake and me?"

"Everywhere I turn lately, people are cheating on their spouses. Why not you, too? Jake's a handsome guy. He's got money. He's clearly interested in you. You're telling me you haven't even been tempted?"

A muscle twitched in Felicia's jaw.

"Most women would swoon for a guy like Jake." God, how I wanted to stop talking. But I'd opened the floodgates now and the words kept spilling out. "It would make sense if you felt it, too. You two are out there, pulling stakeouts in dark cars. Can you blame me for being suspicious?"

"I can't believe I'm hearing this," she said. "You honestly believe I would cheat on you? With Jake, no less?"

"It crossed my mind."

"Jesus." She leapt to her feet. "I can't believe you. I thought you trusted me."

"I do," I whined, "but Jake—"

"Don't say anything more, Bubba. You're just digging yourself in deeper."

Her eyes suddenly were wet. Felicia doesn't cry often. When she does, it's usually a good signal to go hide in another room.

"I'm going to go take a bath," she said. "I don't want to see you when I come out."

"Now, sweetie—"

"I mean it, Bubba. Stay in your office. Go to The Cruise. But don't be around here tonight. I'm too angry to deal with you right now."

She turned and stalked away.

I jumped to my feet, ready to pursue her, ready to apologize. But my feet got tangled in the sandals she'd left on the kitchen floor and my ankle twinged and I had to pull up short. By the time I limped down the hall to the bathroom, she'd closed the door behind her. It was locked. Water thundered into the tub.

I thought about shouting through the door, asking her to come out so we could discuss it some more, make things right. But she might emerge even madder. I limped away, muttering under my breath about what a freaking moron I can be sometimes.

I retired to my office and drank beer and watched a ball game on the little TV I keep in there. I thought about trying to talk to Felicia after she finished her bath, but she was slamming doors and stomping around and I could tell she was still mad.

I can be chickenshit sometimes. I tell myself it's a matter of discretion being the better part of valor, yadda, yadda, yadda, but it's just fear. I hate confrontations with Felicia. She always wins.

Anyway, I hunkered in my office, listening to her angry footfalls. Eventually, after it was clear she'd gone to bed, I fell asleep on the sofa in my office, the TV silently throwing its scattered light on the room.

It was morning when I awoke. I was still in my rumpled clothes. Matt Lauer and Katie Couric were smiling from the TV, mouthing words without sound. I creaked off the broken-down sofa. I felt headachy from guilt and trepidation and beer.

I braved the kitchen and found a note from Felicia. It looked like the same terse note from Sunday. "I'm at the office."

I sighed and trudged over to the coffeemaker. I'd filled a cup, but hadn't yet taken a sip, when the telephone rang.

Twenty Four

"Hello, Bubba. This is Nancy Chilton."

Oh, shit.

"Hello, Mrs. Chilton. How are you today?"

"I'd be a lot better if you hadn't lost those pictures of my husband."

Ouch. I'd been trying to forget my run-in with Boyd Chilton and the embarrassment of losing film, camera and dignity to a man in his boxer shorts. In fact, I would've liked to forget the Chilton case altogether. But Nancy seemed determined to catch her husband with his pants down, and I was the guy who was supposed to do it.

"Yeah, heh-heh, I'm still recovering from that," I said. "Got a new development?"

"Boyd said as he was leaving this morning that he has to 'work late' tonight. I'm guessing he's going to see his bimbo again. I want you to follow him."

"Tonight, huh?" I thought about my own sweetie, working late all the time with that rat Jake Steele. And how angry she'd gotten when I mentioned my suspicions. Maybe I should be tailing my own wife rather than helping Nancy Chilton.

"Is that a problem? Too busy with your other case to help me out?"

"No, it's not that. Though I have been pretty busy on Andrew Rollins' death."

"I thought that's what you must be up to," she said. "I saw you yesterday here in The Manor, snooping around the Rollins house."

Leave it to the neighborhood gossip to spot me while I was peeping at Charisse's pool. Probably everyone in The Manor knew about it by now.

"I wasn't snooping exactly," I said. "I went there to talk to Charisse, but I heard voices out back, so I went around there to see if she was home."

"And was she?"

"Oh, yeah."

"Was Ed Salisbury there with her?"

That question took me by surprise. I hadn't planned to tell Nancy about Salisbury and Charisse, but apparently she already knew Mystery Meat was spending an unseemly amount of time with Rollins' widow.

"Yeah, he was there. How did you know?"

"That bastard practically lives over there," she said, her voice brittle, "now that Andrew is out of the way."

"You think Salisbury had something to do with the murder?"

Silence. I let it build, waiting. If Nancy knew something, she wouldn't be able to keep her big mouth shut for long.

"I wouldn't be surprised," she said finally. "He and Charisse have been fooling around for months now. Maybe he decided it was time to get Andrew out of the way."

I told her what Romero had said about Meat's airtight alibi, but she just snorted.

"If Ed Salisbury wanted to kill Andrew, he could've done it just before that exercise class," she said. "Or he could've slipped out for a second. He's the kind of guy, so charismatic, he could persuade the whole class to say whatever he wanted."

That seemed unlikely to me. Romero said forty people in that class vouched for Salisbury. Short of mass hypnosis, I couldn't see any way he could've fooled them all.

"What about Charisse?" I asked. "Think she could be behind it?"

"I wouldn't put anything past her," Nancy said. "She's evil, through and through. Remember how she greeted you with a gun in her hand?"

Like I could forget.

"She's capable of killing," she continued. "I'm sure of it. But maybe she and Ed found someone else to do the killing for them. Did you think of that?"

"Sure, but—"

"I think the police are making a mistake if they don't suspect Ed Salisbury," she said. "He's the kind of person who looks out only for himself. No loyalty. No scruples."

This was beginning to sound like a diatribe.

"How do you know so much about Salisbury?"

"Trust me, I know him," she said. "I know his type. Chasing after young Charisse even though she's married to his boss. He's no better than she is."

"Sounds like you've given this a lot of thought."

"Not really. I'm just tired of cheaters getting away with it. I guess that's why I'm so set on catching Boyd."

Which was where I had come in.

"Okay, Mrs. Chilton. I'll trail your husband tonight, see what I can turn up."

"Catch him in the act, Bubba. I need proof so my lawyer can nail him to the wall."

"Yes, ma'am."

I was ready to hang up and go back to my cooling coffee.

"And Bubba?"

"Uh-huh?"

"If you're serious about finding Andrew's killer, I'd suggest you stay after Salisbury. I'm sure he's behind it all."

"Okay. Thanks for the advice. I will."

I promised to call her the next day with a report on Boyd, and she let me hang up.

I took a sip of my coffee—finally—and was hunting around the living room for the morning *Gazette* when the phone rang again.

With a heavy sigh, I picked up the receiver, expecting it to be Nancy Chilton with more thoughts on how I should do my job.

"Bubba? It's Melvin Haywood."

Whoa.

"Good morning, Mr. Haywood. How are you?"

"Not so good, Bubba. I couldn't sleep all night, thinking about being wanted by the police. I'd better come back to Albuquerque and turn myself in."

For an instant, I almost agreed. If Haywood surrendered to the cops, then determining whether he was Rollins' killer became their problem instead of mine. Lord knows I was sick of thinking about who killed Andrew Rollins. But if I let Haywood turn himself in, then I wouldn't have done my job. And I wouldn't get paid.

"No, you don't want to do that," I said. "Not yet. I think I'm onto something."

"You know who killed Rollins?"

"I've got some ideas."

I told him that Salisbury and Charisse had been fooling

around before (and certainly after) Rollins was killed.

"Hmm. That looks suspicious, doesn't it?"

"Does to me. The cops don't seem too interested yet. Salisbury's got a solid alibi."

"Unlike me," Haywood interjected.

"Right, but maybe he got a buddy to kill Rollins. Or maybe Charisse sneaked into the clinic and did it herself."

"Charisse? You think she's capable of something like that?"

Nancy Chilton's words ran through my mind as I pictured Charisse in her red bikini, waving a pistol at me.

"I'm beginning to think so, yeah."

"My Lord." Haywood paused. "But how will you prove it, Bubba? Can you make them confess or something?"

"I'm not sure." A confession probably was out of the question, but I didn't want to say so. What I needed was some leverage, some way to pry evidence out of Salisbury or Charisse.

"Well," Haywood said, "if you're going to force something out of them, today's the day. I'm coming back to Albuquerque in the morning, either way."

"What if I don't have anything by then?"

"Then I'll go to the police. Tell them I've been out of town the whole time. Maybe they'll listen to reason."

That didn't sound like any of the cops I knew—except maybe Romero—but perhaps Haywood was more idealistic than me.

"You're flying in?" I asked.

"I'm arriving on America West at eleven. Flight two-two-seven."

"I'll meet you at the airport. If I've got something by then, I can fill you in and you can decide whether to go to the cops. If I don't have anything and you still want to turn yourself in, I'll go with you, see if I can grease the skids."

"That's forward-thinking of you, Bubba. But I'll probably need a lawyer more than a private eye at that point."

"Maybe it won't come to that. I might solve the case by then."

Haywood hesitated and I guessed he was looking at a clock. "That only gives you twenty-four hours."

And during that twenty-four hours, I also had to tail Boyd Chilton and patch things up with Felicia. But Haywood didn't need to know all that. He only needed to believe that I might be able to get him out of this fix.

"I'll do my best," I pledged.

"I know you will, Bubba. See you tomorrow."

Damn. Twenty-four hours to find a killer. And I hadn't even had a full dose of caffeine yet. I slugged down my coffee, but it had gone stone-cold and I spat it into the sink. I looked at the kitchen clock, then hurried off to the shower.

I showered and shaved and brushed and dressed in record time. I wolfed down food and fresh coffee. Then I was ready to go track down a killer.

Only one more thing I needed before I left the house. I got my Smith & Wesson .38-caliber revolver from a locked drawer in my desk.

Time to talk to Ed Salisbury. This time, I'd be ready.

Twenty Five

Andrew Rollins' death hadn't yet made a dent in business at the clinic. The parking lot was full of shiny, expensive cars. I parked the Ram on a nearby side street, stuffed the pistol into my waistband under my loose shirt and strolled over to the clinic entrance.

Inside, the waiting room was jammed. But I got lucky. Nurse Wyborn wasn't in the window that connected to the reception office. In fact, no one was visible through the window. I nodded and smiled at the patients as I stepped over their crutches to the door to the inner offices.

Lucky again. The hall was empty, though I could hear voices behind some of the closed doors. I hotfooted it down the hall, peeking in doors. In one room, a female physical therapist was working over some old woman's knee. They both swiveled their heads to look at me and I said, "Oops. Wrong room." Smiled as I closed the door.

My heart was thumping. If I opened the wrong door and found myself face to ugly face with Nurse Wyborn, I'd probably wet my pants.

A couple of empty examination rooms later, I came to two facing doors at the end of the hall. Both were labeled "Exercise Room." I listened at the door to my right and heard the tromp of feet, punctuated by the occasional groan. A woman's chirpy voice exhorted clients to exercise harder, which led me to believe Mystery Meat wasn't in there with them. If he was in there, he'd be doing the shouting, right?

I listened at the other door and heard nothing. I swung the door open, not expecting to find anyone, and there was Salisbury standing in the middle of the room.

He was alone, except for his reflected image, which looked back at him from mirrored walls. Exercise equipment—weight machines, medicine balls and various other torture devices—ringed the room. Salisbury stood among racks of barbells and chrome dumbbells. His hands were full of yellow "Crime Scene" tape and I guessed that this was the place where Andrew Rollins bought the farm. He looked as if he was cleaning up, getting rid of any sign of the police, so the gym could be used again. A solid-looking door was set into the far wall, probably a service entrance for hauling in equipment. That door gave me an idea.

I surmised all this in the few seconds before Mystery Meat looked up and our eyes met. He scowled at the sight of me. I gulped.

"The fuck do you want?"

I tried smiling. It didn't take.

"How did you get in here?"

I pushed through the door and flinched as it swung closed behind me.

"I let myself in," I said casually. "You really ought to have somebody posted at that reception area out front. Anybody could walk in here."

His jaw clenched. He was dressed all in white—sweatpants and a tight T-shirt and sneakers—and it provided a nice contrast as his face darkened. He wadded the yellow

tape into a ball and threw it angrily at a trash can in the corner. The shot rimmed out, which made me grin. Then I
reminded myself that Mystery Meat's athletic specialty had
been maiming quarterbacks, not shooting baskets.

"So this is where Dr. Rollins was killed? Right about
where you're standing?"

He squinted at me, didn't answer. The muscles in his
arms rippled under his skin. Looked like live animals were
moving around under there.

"And you were where when it happened? Just across the
hall?"

"What the hell are you talking about?"

"Just trying to figure out how you did it."

"Did what?"

"Killed your boss."

That tore it. His hands reached toward me, flexing into
claws, and he started my way. We were only about twelve
feet apart, but I was quicker. The Smith & Wesson appeared
in my hand and Salisbury pulled up short.

"You might be tough," I said confidently, "but you sure
as hell ain't bulletproof. Just stay where you are."

He did as he was told, but he looked as if he were wondering how many bullets I could put into him before he
could get his hands on me. I wondered the same thing, and
whether two or three slugs would be enough to bring
down a man that size.

He cocked an eyebrow and said, "Guess we're going to
talk."

"Guess we are. You might have the police bamboozled,
but I think you killed Rollins. Or had him killed."

"Why would I do that? The man saved my life."

"How do you mean?"

"I came out of the NFL with two knees so fucked up, everyone said I'd be in a wheelchair the rest of my life. Andrew put me back together. He got me through physical therapist school, gave me a job. I owed him everything. Why would I kill him?"

The pistol was heavy. I steadied it with my other hand, kept it pointed at his chest. If anything would make him come charging at me, it would be what I said next.

"Because you're screwing his wife."

Mystery Meat grimaced. He looked as if he wanted to throttle me.

"The police already know about Charisse and me," he said finally.

"I know they do. And, lucky you, they're choosing to ignore it. But I think you have a pretty good motive. Especially since Charisse stands to inherit this clinic."

It didn't seem possible that Salisbury's face could get any redder, but it did. I wondered what all this anger was doing to his blood pressure. I half-expected blood to spurt out the top of his head like lava from a volcano.

"You don't know shit," he growled. "I've got witnesses who say I didn't do it."

"Then tell me how you managed it. Did Charisse come through that back door over there and kill him? Or did you hire somebody to do it?"

He clamped his mouth shut, which made his thick mustache bristle.

I circled away from the hall door, keeping my distance from him, glancing down to keep from tripping over exercise gear scattered around the floor.

"Come on, Meat. Tell me how it went down. I'll prove it one way or the other."

"You can't prove dick."

"No? Then let's hear a denial."

"Go to hell," he snarled.

"You first. I bet there's a special section set aside for men who kill their lovers' husbands."

He took a step toward me, but I waggled the pistol and said, "Uh-uh-uh. I'll shoot."

"You don't have the balls."

I lowered the angle of the gun, pointing it toward his crotch.

"Take another step, and you won't have any."

That stopped him.

I have to admit, I was beginning to enjoy this. After the way Mystery Meat had roughed me up—twice—it felt good to have the upper hand.

Naturally, that's when all hell broke loose. The hall door swung open. Nurse Hildegarde Wyborn's bulk filled the doorway. She looked at Meat, then followed his gaze to where I stood, holding a pistol. Her face blanched.

I wanted to swing the pistol toward her, tell her to come in and join the conversation. But I was afraid to move the gun off Meat, even for a second. He looked ready to spring.

"Hold it right there!" I shouted at the nurse. But it was too late. She wheeled away from the door, damned fast for a fat lady, and ran off down the hall. As the door was closing behind her, Meat shouted, "Call the cops, Hildy!"

He turned back to me with a smirk. "Guess who's in trouble now."

"I'll just be leaving. You stay right where you are."

I edged away, keeping the gun pointed at him until I reached the back door.

"You're never going to get away with this," he muttered.

"Up yours, buddy." I smiled at him and turned the doorknob.

As I'd figured, the door opened to the outdoors. I stepped into an asphalt alley behind the clinic. The door was on a pneumatic hinge and it closed ever so slowly. I watched the door, making sure Meat wasn't following, until it was nearly shut. Then I turned to run like hell.

Before I'd taken two steps, I heard a loud crack from inside the exercise room. Sounded like a gunshot. That gave wings to my feet. I hobbled down the alley and around the corner and across the parking lot to the Ram. I jumped inside and cranked up the engine and got out of there fast, expecting the whole time to hear sirens screaming.

Only when I was several blocks away did I catch my breath. And then I had a moment to wonder: What was that noise inside the gym? Meat certainly hadn't had a gun in there. I wondered whether the nurse had run off to fetch a pistol rather than call the cops. Had she been trying to shoot me?

I tried to put it out of my mind as I drove aimlessly through the old residential neighborhoods south of Lomas Boulevard. I needed to re-examine my conversation with Mystery Meat for clues. And I needed to keep moving. Because Meat and Nurse Wyborn no doubt had called the cops by now. And if the police caught up to me before I finished solving the murder, I'd have a lot of explaining to do. You can't just point guns at people and get away with it. Not unless you can give the cops something better than an assault-with-a-deadly-weapon rap to keep them busy.

And so far, I had zilch.

Twenty Six

I put a lot of miles on the Ram that hot afternoon, cruising around the city. I figured it wasn't safe to go home if the cops were looking for me, and I didn't have any other place to go. I used my cell phone to try to reach Romero, thinking I could explain what had happened, but he wasn't available. I tried to call Felicia, but couldn't reach her. I even tried to call Nancy Chilton to check for any new word about Boyd, but she wasn't home. I had to ask myself why I even bothered to own a cell phone.

Finally, it was nearing five o'clock and I had somewhere to be. I parked on the sorority house hill above Boyd's dealership and watched for him to leave in his big gold Cadillac.

The arrangement hadn't changed. The Caddie still was parked in the slot nearest the dealership's back door. Boyd still came through it a few minutes after five, wearing his white cowboy hat. Then he was behind the wheel and I was hauling ass back to University Boulevard to chase after him.

This time, I got caught by traffic long enough that Boyd passed me, going south. He'd gone north last time, headed for his bimbo's apartment, and I wondered whether he had another girlfriend in a different part of town.

I followed him east on Central Avenue to the parking lot of a country-western joint called the Stumble Inn. He locked up the Cadillac and strolled inside, not a care in the world. I sat in the truck, wondering what to do next.

I'd been inside the Stumble Inn before. It's a big, smoky, windowless place with a long wooden bar and sawdust on the floor. Cowboys and cowgirls circle the floor like dervishes, doing complicated maneuvers with their feet.

The Stumble Inn would be a nice spot for an old cowboy like Boyd Chilton to meet his girlfriend at night. Dark and crowded enough that they could get lost in there, not have to worry about being spotted by one of Nancy's tennis-club friends. But it was broad daylight and the parking lot was maybe one-third full. Just the day drinkers and the happy hour hounds.

I knew I had to go inside to keep an eye on Boyd, but that made me nervous. He'd gotten a good look at me outside his girlfriend's apartment. If he spotted me in the bar, it could mean trouble.

I'm not without my resources. I dug around in the Ram until I came up with a disguise. A baseball cap that said "Buttram's Hog Feed" on the front should make me fit right in with the cowboy crowd, and it would hide the upper part of my face under its bill. In the glove compartment, I had an item I'd picked up at a costume shop: A Fu Manchu mustache that came with its own adhesive. I sat tall in the seat so I could see in the mirror and carefully pressed the mustache into place. It changed my appearance tremendously. I looked just like the kind of hick who'd kick up his heels at the Stumble Inn.

I locked my pistol in the glove compartment and went inside the bar, walking with the rolling amble that cowboys use because they've spent too much time in a saddle.

There was no doorman at this hour, which was just as well because darkness and smoke and wailing music swamped me. I stepped to one side of the door and took a moment to get my bearings.

Only a few couples drag-assed around the dance floor to recorded Travis Tritt. Drums and amps and cables and other gear sat on the stage, hinting at a live performance to come, and I just prayed Boyd would be done here before some local caterwaulers cranked up the country. A deejay occupied a booth to one side of the stage, his hands full of compact discs as he sorted for the next selection. He wore a white straw cowboy hat, like many of the men in the place. A few wore caps like mine, which comforted me.

I spotted Boyd Chilton to the left of the big dance floor, sitting at the head of a long table. Four other guys sat with him. They were hatless and wore dress shirts with the sleeves rolled up and loosened ties and cheesey smiles. Salesmen. I could smell them all the way across the room. Boyd wasn't meeting a girlfriend here. He was conducting a sales meeting. Shit.

I edged around the far side of the room, pausing at the bar long enough to order a longneck beer. The leather-faced bartender looked at me funny, which caused my hand to shoot up to my face to check on the mustache. The glue seemed to be holding. Hell, maybe the bartender looked at everybody that way. Or maybe something else in my demeanor gave me away. The sweat on my brow. The fact I was wearing sneakers instead of boots. I paid for my beer and moseyed away from him.

I wanted a table within earshot of Boyd, but one that wouldn't put me directly in his line of sight. I didn't have enough faith in my disguise to think he wouldn't recognize me, given the chance. I circled around behind him, which required crossing the dance floor near the stage, and found a table in the corner. I couldn't see Boyd's face from this position, but I could hear his loud voice and joshing laugh.

I watched the table for the duration of my beer, and was wondering whether to risk another trip to the bar when a pair of black slacks appeared beside my table.

"Bubba?"

I chanced a glimpse out from under the bill of my cap to look up at the man's face. Jake Steele, in the flesh. Wearing a black suit over a lavender polo shirt. Couldn't have looked more out of place at the Stumble Inn if he'd been wearing scuba gear. What the shit was he doing here? And how had he recognized me?

I put a finger to my lips to shush him and found that the Fu Manchu was hanging loose on one side. Oh. I smoothed it back into place, pressing hard to secure it.

Jake Steele made himself at home at my table.

"What are you doing here, done up like that?" he asked.

I made shushing gestures at him. "I'm on a stakeout," I whispered. "This—" I checked the mustache again. "—is supposed to be a disguise."

Steele's face split in a movie-star grin. "Work a lot better if it wasn't hanging down in your beer."

I made a face at him, which caused the mustache to slip again. I mooshed it back into place, wishing for a mirror so I could make sure it was on straight. And wishing Jake Steele would get the hell away from me.

"What are you doing in a place like this?" I asked.

He chuckled manfully. "Guess you could say I'm on stakeout, too. Part of the project Felicia and I are sharing."

I felt my eyes narrow. The project wasn't all this lounge

lizard wanted to share with Felicia. I was sure of that. My earlier jealous thoughts crowded my brain, making it hard to be nice to him. I glanced around the Stumble Inn to make sure Felicia wasn't there somewhere. I didn't think I could stand that.

"Is this how it goes?" I asked him. "Felicia's slaving away back at the office, while you hang out in bars?"

The grin slid off his face. "I'm working. I don't even get to have a beer, unlike some people."

I'd just been hankering for another beer, but I remembered how I'd drunk myself into oblivion the last time I'd seen Steele.

"Who are you here watching?" he asked.

I didn't want to say Boyd Chilton's name. Even in a noisy bar, people respond to hearing their own names. I didn't want Boyd turning around, looking at me. I lifted my chin in Boyd's direction without saying a word.

"Really?" Steele laughed. "Me, too."

"What?"

"He's one of the guys on our list," he said. "Those are his top salesmen."

Ah, so I'd gotten that right.

"I heard they were meeting here this evening, so I thought I'd eavesdrop."

"What makes you think they'd come to a place like this to talk about dirty deals?"

Jake shrugged. "More likely to do it at a noisy bar than in the office where others might hear. So far, though, it looks like they're just here to drink beer."

A buxom waitress brought more beers to their table as Jake spoke. The salesmen leered and jeered. She didn't bat an eye. Wait tables in a joint like this, you hear all the lines.

"Look, Jake," I murmured, "I don't mean to be rude, but could you move to another table? I don't want him looking over here."

"He doesn't know me," Jake said.

"Well, he's seen me before. That's why I'm wearing this stupid disguise."

"Speaking of which, your mustache is falling off again."

"Damn." I frantically put the fuzzy worm back in place under my nose. "I guess the glue's worn out. It's been in a glove compartment for a long time. This heat—"

"Why are you tailing him?" Jake interrupted.

"Can't say."

"You working with Felicia?"

"Hell, no. I've got a regular client. Doesn't have anything to do with the *Gazette*."

Jake ran a hand back over his perfect black hair. He was smiling again.

"Let me think," he said. "Why would a private eye be following Boyd Chilton? Maybe because he screws around on his wife?"

I winced. "You want to keep your voice down? You're going to ruin everything."

I looked away, trying to ignore him, still hoping he'd go away. One of the salesmen had his eyes on me. He leaned over to Boyd Chilton and pointed in my direction.

Uh-oh.

I lowered my head, trying to hide behind the visor of the cap, but I heard Chilton curse loudly and chair legs scrape on the floor. Oh, shit, here they come.

It occurred to me it was a good thing Jake was there. Not likely that Boyd Chilton would cause too big a scene with a reporter for the local newspaper sitting right there. I glanced over Jake's way, only to find an empty chair. He'd vanished, like smoke, like a rainbow, like your lap does when you stand up. I wheeled around, searching for him, but he was nowhere to be found.

Of course, I couldn't see much. My view was blocked by Boyd Chilton and his four salesmen. They looked angry. Chilton's face was as red as my truck. Speaking of my truck, that was exactly where I wanted to be right now.

I kept my seat. I didn't want to provoke them. I wondered how they had spotted me. I wondered how Jake Steele had vanished. I wondered how the hell I was going to get out of this mess without enduring some serious bodily harm.

Chilton reached a meaty hand across the table toward me. I flinched, but there was nowhere to go, and he grabbed the end of the Fu Manchu and yanked it off my face. Ouch. The sudden sting made me cover my mouth with both hands.

Boyd Chilton wagged the mustache under the end of my nose. It looked like he was flinging around somebody's eyebrow.

"What the hell is this?" he demanded. "You following me again?"

Now, see, if I hadn't bothered with the disguise, I could've denied it. Could've claimed I was an innocent bystander, just another guy who'd stopped at the Stumble Inn for a beer. Could've claimed it was a case of mistaken identity, that I'd never seen Boyd Chilton before in my life. But he held in his fat fingers evidence to the contrary. Your Average Joe doesn't don a fake mustache for an afternoon beer in a cowboy joint.

"I—"

"What are you, a private snoop?" he asked. "Who hired you?"

I clearly wasn't going to get a word in edgewise, so I just shook my head.

Boyd cursed. The salesmen shifted on either side of him. They looked a lot bigger looming over me than they had lounging around the table. And they looked eager for trouble.

I peeked between them, hoping for a bouncer, a bartender, a waitress alert enough to sense impending violence. Nobody. We were back in a corner, hidden away as I had wanted, and I could undergo a severe beating before anybody noticed me squealing over the loud music.

"I ought to kick your ass all over this place," Boyd snarled.

Diversions ran through my mind. I could throw my empty beer bottle at him. Use the distraction to wheel out of my chair and get into some sort of defensive position. I've been in bar fights before. I know the secret is to hit people with whatever's handy. No sense breaking your fist on some jerk's jawbone when ashtrays are right there.

But it was futility. Five of them and only one of me. I might go down fighting, but I'd still go down. I feared I was about to have some close personal interaction with Boyd's cowboy boots.

The music suddenly stopped. A silence fell over the saloon, so abrupt it distracted Boyd and his boys. They turned to look. Peeking between them, I spied two uniformed cops standing just inside the door, talking to the leathery bartender.

Rarely have I been so glad to see our boys in blue.

One of the cops cleared his throat and said, loudly enough to be heard all over the bar, "We're looking for a man named Wilton Mabry."

My heart rose in my throat. I was rescued. No way Boyd and his salesmen could attack now. I stood and waved at the cops. Boyd glared at me, looked like he was filing my name away for future use. Fine by me. The cavalry had arrived, and I was safe for now.

Boyd and his salesmen melted away as the cops approached. The cops were young guys, both wearing thin mustaches that didn't require glue. They were nearly identical, except one was about six inches taller than the other. Each had a hand on the butt of his pistol. Again, fine by me. They could fire warning shots if they wanted to. Anything to scare off Boyd Chilton.

The taller of the two said, "You're Wilton Mabry? Drive that red Dodge truck out in the parking lot?"

I nodded eagerly. "You can call me Bubba."

"Okay, Bubba. You're under arrest."

All the air went out of me. I sputtered and stuttered while the other cop gestured me out from behind the table and pulled handcuffs from his belt.

"On what charge?" I finally managed.

"Attempted murder."

"What? I didn't try to kill anybody!"

"Tell them about it downtown," the tall cop said as the other clinked the cuffs around my wrists.

They led me away. The music resumed before we even reached the door, but nobody was dancing. They all stared at me. And there, near the door, was Boyd Chilton, smirking. He made his hand into a fat pistol and dropped his thumb at me.

Bang. You're going to jail.

Twenty Seven

Now if I had a client in this same situation, my advice would be succinct—shut the fuck up. Don't say a word until you've got a lawyer sitting next to you. It's the smart thing to do. But nobody's ever accused me of being smart.

I talked all the way out the door and into the parking lot, demanding that the cops tell me what it was all about, who I'd allegedly tried to murder, what's the meaning of this, etc. They kept their faces impassive and herded me toward their waiting patrol car.

Finally, something clicked in my head, and I said, "Look, if this is about what happened at the Rollins clinic, I didn't attempt to murder anybody there. I just used the gun to protect myself from Ed Salisbury, who's already whipped up on me twice—"

Their eyes lit up at the mention of the clinic. Uh-oh.

"You pointed a gun at Salisbury?" the taller cop asked.

"Yeah, but I didn't pull the trigger. I never had any intention—"

"Where is that gun now?"

"It's in my truck, but—"

"Mind if we take it in with us?"

Oh, shit, what had I done?

I balked. They made noises about getting a search warrant. I balked again. The shorter cop made a crack about how they couldn't guarantee I'd get my truck back in pristine condition. I relented. We went and got the pistol out of the glove compartment. They lifted it out with a pencil through the trigger guard and put it in a plastic bag.

"That gun hasn't been fired in months," I said.

"We'll leave that to the lab guys," the taller cop said. And they hustled me off to the squad car.

I asked more questions on the way downtown, carefully posed questions that wouldn't give anything else away, but the cops were mum.

When we reached the police station, they took me straight up to the third floor and through a door labeled "Crimes Against Persons." I knew one or two cops in that division, but I'd never seen the plainclothes one, Sgt. Irwin Goff, who escorted me into a tiny interview room and hooked my handcuffs to a straight-backed metal chair.

Goff was an African-American guy, maybe thirty years old, with the standard-issue cop mustache. I think half the force wears a clipped, military-style soup-strainer. The cop shop sometimes resembles a gay bar. Goff also sported a shaved head and an expensive-looking blue suit. All in all, he resembled Montel Williams, and I'd wager he secretly admired the resemblance every morning when he looked in the mirror.

Once he was settled across the narrow table from me, he turned on a tape recorder and said, "Mr. Mabry, do you know why you're under arrest?"

His voice was smooth and deep. Sort of like Montel's. His face betrayed nothing. I'm sure that mine, on the other hand, was sweaty and wild-eyed and beet red. My blood pounded in my ears and my bowels felt loose. On top of everything else, my nose itched like crazy and I couldn't do anything about it with my hands cuffed behind my back.

"No, I don't," I proclaimed. "I told those cops I never tried to kill anybody—"

He held up a well-manicured hand. "Did they read you your rights?"

"Yeah, but—"

"And you understand those rights?"

"Sure, but I want to know—"

"Let me ask the questions, all right?"

I clammed up and nodded.

"Okay, do you want a lawyer here now?"

I thought this over. Surely I could get this sorted out on my own. It's all just a big mistake, right? I thought about my pitifully small bank account and how much an attorney would cost and said, "Not yet. Let's see if we can't resolve this first."

"All right." A smile played around his lips. Clearly, he thought I'd just screwed up. I straightened in my chair, tried to clear my head. This guy looked intelligent and experienced and smooth. I needed to be on my toes.

"Did you visit the Rollins Sports Medicine Clinic this morning?" he asked.

"Yes, I did."

"And, once there, did you sneak past the front desk and go to an exercise room in the rear of the building?"

"I didn't exactly 'sneak.' There was no one at the front desk—"

"But you went to the exercise room?"

I nodded. He instructed me to answer out loud and gestured at the tape recorder. I said, "Yes."

"Good. And there you met with Edward Salisbury?"

"He was there. He wasn't too happy to see me."

"Why's that?"

"Because he's guilty, that's why. Twice, he's assaulted me when I've tried to ask questions—"

His eyebrows rose, but he didn't let me finish. "Did you report these assaults?"

"No."

"I see. But because of these assaults, you had a grudge against Mr. Salisbury?"

"I wouldn't say that."

Again with the almost-smile. I could tell we'd be coming back to that question.

"You produced a gun once you were face-to-face with Mr. Salisbury, did you not?"

I suddenly saw through Goff. "Did you not" gave him away. He was one of those cops who was working his way through law school. An up-and-comer, trying to make a reputation. A future district attorney. Oh, boy. Just what I didn't need. I needed a world-weary old-timer like Romero, somebody who's heard it all. They, at least, would cut to the freaking chase rather than toying around with lawyer-speak.

"Sure, I had a gun. Like I said, he'd assaulted me. I didn't want him to do it again."

He nodded, looked like he wasn't really listening. I realized then I wasn't talking to him. I was talking to the tape recorder that sat on the table between us, as black and shiny and deadly as a snake.

"I wanted to talk to Salisbury," I said, aware that I was speaking clearly and irrevocably. "I believe he's guilty of murder and I was trying to make him confess."

"By holding a gun on him?"

I recognized how stupid that looked in retrospect. "I was asking him questions."

"And did he answer those questions to your satisfaction?"

More lawyer-speak. I was really starting to dislike this guy. I shook my head, then remembered the tape recorder and said, "No."

"And a nurse at the clinic, a—" He checked his notes. "—Hildegarde Wyborn, opened the door about that time."

"Right."

"What happened next?"

"She ran off to call the police, so I thought I'd better leave."

"And that's when you shot Mr. Salisbury?"

He asked it in an off-hand manner, like he thought he had me lulled into a question-and-answer rhythm and I would just go along. My reaction was somewhat different. I tried to leap to my feet, but the handcuffs yanked me back into place.

Then it hit me. That loud crack as I was hurrying away from the clinic. It had been a gunshot. Somebody shot Ed Salisbury while I was going the other direction, my gun in my hand.

Holy guacamole, it looked like I'd done it. Nurse Wyborn had seen me holding a gun on Mystery Meat. Naturally, they thought I did it. Hell, given the evidence, I would've thought I was guilty. But, as much as I might've wanted to wing Salisbury, I was certain I hadn't pulled the trigger.

"Hell, no," I said, once I had it sorted out. "I didn't shoot anybody."

"You're holding a gun on a man. The man is shot. But

you didn't do it."

I told him how I'd left by the back door, how I'd heard the shot, but didn't realize at the time that anyone had been hit. He nodded along, not believing a word of it.

"Test my gun," I said. "It hasn't been fired. Test my hands. You won't find any gunpowder residue."

He smiled. "You've had plenty of time to clean your hands. We're testing your gun, but how do we know it's the same one you used at the clinic? You voluntarily surrendered it."

"I was trying to be cooperative!"

"Maybe you ditched the gun you used, then handed over this one, thinking it would get you off."

"It's the only gun I own!"

I sounded shrill in my own ears. It was a shock, being hauled in this way and accused of shooting an unarmed Meat. I wasn't handling it well.

I took a deep breath and said, "I'll take that lawyer now."

He smiled and got to his feet. Clearly, he thought he had me nailed. He fetched a phone from an outer office and plugged it into the wall. I called my lawyer, got an answering machine. Shit. It was after-hours. Good luck finding an attorney in the evening. I didn't even know his home number.

"How about this," I offered to Goff, "could you get Lieutenant Romero down here? From Homicide? He's a friend of mine. He'll tell you I'd never do something like this."

Goff resisted at first, but when I made it clear I wasn't saying another word until I had either a lawyer or Romero, he summoned the lieutenant.

Romero looked pissed when he arrived, and his expres-

sion didn't improve as we walked through my story again.
When I was done, he said, "This looks bad, Bubba."

"I know, but I didn't do it. You can vouch for me. I came
to you, telling you I thought Salisbury killed Rollins."

"Yeah, and I told you he had an alibi."

"Still, I didn't have any reason to shoot him."

"He beat you up, right? Twice?"

"Not 'beat up' exactly. He sort of threw me through the
air."

"So you were angry at him?"

"Now you're sounding like this guy." I jerked my head
toward Goff, who glowered at me. He didn't like sharing
his glory with Romero. Probably trying for a new record on
how quickly an attempted murder could be resolved. We
were just holding him up.

"I wasn't pissed," I said. "I was trying to solve a crime."

"By committing another one?"

"I didn't shoot him!"

"But even holding a gun on him, that's assault with a
deadly weapon."

He had me there.

"You should know better, Bubba."

I hung my head. What could I say? He was right. I'd
thought I could bull my way through, scare a confession
out of Mystery Meat. Now Meat was in the hospital and I
was in deep shit.

"How is Salisbury?" I asked. "He hurt bad?"

"He's out of surgery over at Lovelace," Goff said. "Still
unconscious, but they got the bullet out. He'll pull through.
Lucky for you."

Yeah, lucky for me. Otherwise, I'd be facing a murder
rap.

"By the way," I said, "where did I allegedly shoot him?"

A fire came into Goff's eyes. "In the back."

"Now, see, there's some proof. He was facing me when I went out that door. No way I could've shot him in the back."

Goff had been waiting in a corner, letting Romero do the questioning, but now he leaned across the table to get in my face.

"Anybody see that?" he asked.

My "no" sounded meek in my own ears.

"Then how do you expect us to believe it?"

Romero stood up. "Sergeant, can I see you outside?"

They closed the door behind them, but the door had a narrow window in it and I watched Romero argue with the younger man. I hoped he was trying to talk him out of pressing charges, and I hoped he was persuasive as hell. Their talk went on a long time. When it was over, Romero wheeled and vanished from view. That didn't bode well.

Goff came back inside, turned the tape recorder back on.

"I think we've got enough evidence to charge you with attempted murder," he said firmly. "You'll now be booked into the county jail."

"You've got it all wrong," I said.

"We'll let the district attorney's office sort it out."

"I can make bail, right?"

"That'll be up to a judge. You'll have an initial hearing in the morning."

"In the morning? Are you saying I've got to spend the night in jail?"

He smiled again. "That's right."

All the blood rushed out of my head. I felt faint. I'm afraid of many things in this world—snakes, heights, cancer, needles, Felicia—but jail is my worst fear of all. Being stuck in a holding pen with real criminals, guys who'd just as soon rape you as say "hello," guys who maybe really had shot somebody, scared me to death.

I think I went into a sort of shock. I remember being fingerprinted and photographed. I remember losing my clothes and being forced to wear an orange inmate jumpsuit. At the time, it all seemed to be happening to somebody else. Like I was watching it on TV. Through a fog.

And then I was in jail. Sitting off in a corner by myself, sweating and dizzy, watching the other inmates mill around the big open dayroom, waiting for one to attack. Nobody paid any attention to me. They were busy with their own problems, or playing cards with their buddies or watching TV. I sat all alone, ignored, frightened and—damn it!—innocent. And nobody gave a shit.

After an hour or two, I finally came to my senses enough to request a phone call. Felicia had no idea where I was. A bored guard let me call her after I assured him it was a local call. She wasn't home.

"Felicia, it's me," I told the answering machine. "I'm in jail. It's a long story. Do something to get me out of here. Please."

I hung up. The guard smirked as I slipped back through the inmates to my hidey-hole in the corner.

Felicia wasn't home. Probably working late again. With Jake Steele. That gave me something else to chew on while I sat up all night, afraid to sleep.

Twenty Eight

Felicia bailed me out the next morning. She was there in the courtroom when I had my preliminary hearing, ready with a twitchy bail bondsman named "Lightning Lenny" Velasquez as soon as the judge dropped the gavel on my fifty-thousand-dollar bond. She'd already filled out the forms to get the bail, using our house as collateral. "Lightning Lenny" lived up to his advertising motto: "Back on the streets in a flash." Within an hour, I was in my own clothes and riding eastward in Felicia's Toyota, into the dazzling summer sun.

My eyes were scratchy and my head hurt and all I wanted was to go home and crawl into my own bed for several days. Naturally, Felicia was having none of that. She had to hear all about my arrest. She'd sat up much of the night, too, after she got my message, waiting on daylight and my court hearing, so she felt entitled. I didn't feel like telling it again, but she'd rescued me from jail. It was the least I could do.

By the time I finished, she was shaking her head in wonder.

"I don't know how you get yourself into these things, Bubba."

"By acting stupid. I shouldn't have gone to that clinic packing a pistol."

She managed a wry smile. "You'd probably gotten beat up again if you hadn't."

"A beating would've been better than this. I'm in real trouble this time. I mean, I think I'll get off eventually, but it's going to cost us a bundle."

She reached over and patted my knee. "Don't worry, Bubba. We'll get it straightened out. We'll sic a lawyer on them. Sounds to me like this case is full of holes."

"I'm lucky I'm not full of holes, spending the night in jail."

"Did anybody threaten you?"

"No. I sat up all night, expecting something. But my fellow inmates ignored me."

"They've got their own problems."

"I wasn't taking any chances. I didn't want to become one of those prison rape cases you see on TV."

"Nobody tried to rape you, huh?" She was trying not to grin. "Guess you weren't their type. Must be tough, getting passed over by a bunch of desperadoes."

I didn't find this funny.

"Didn't they even ask you to dance?"

"I was a wallflower," I said tightly.

I told her I'd left my truck in the parking lot of the Stumble Inn, so she steered over to Central Avenue rather than go straight home.

"Better not let your truck sit there any longer," she said. "Assuming somebody hasn't already stripped it."

Thinking back to the Stumble Inn reminded me of something I hadn't mentioned.

"Jake Steele was at the bar when I was arrested."

"He was?"

"Yeah. He sat at my table, told me he was trailing Boyd Chilton, too. But as soon as the trouble started, he evaporated."

"I'm not surprised," she said. "I can't imagine Jake in a bar fight. Plus, he's trying to stay undercover until we finish our project."

She was apologizing for him! I couldn't believe it. The rat vanished when I could've used someone watching my back, then did nothing when the cops hauled me away.

"Did you see him last night?" I asked. "Did he even mention I'd been arrested?"

"He didn't say anything. Guess he slipped out before the cops busted you."

I doubted that. I'd bet he was hanging around in the shadows somewhere, handsomely grinning as he watched me be handcuffed. And naturally he wouldn't tell Felicia. Let me stew in jail all night. He probably thought that would give him more time to make passes at my wife.

"I don't understand what you see in that guy," I grumbled.

She frowned. "You're not going to start that again, are you? I don't *see* anything in him. I don't even like him that much, to tell you the truth. We're co-workers, that's all. I didn't choose him for this project. The editors stuck me with him. Frankly, I would've been happier doing the whole thing alone. You know I hate to share a byline."

I nodded. That much was true.

"He's not even a very good reporter," she continued. "I've been carrying him through this whole investigation."

"He's got the hots for you, though," I said. "I can tell."

She rolled her eyes. "I doubt that. And even if it's true, he's wasting his time. I'm not interested. I've got all the man I can handle right here."

She patted my knee again. This time, she let her hand rest there.

"Sorry I mentioned it," I said after a while. "I'm not myself. I need some sleep."

"Of course you do. You've been through an ordeal."

Ah, some sympathy. That's what I needed more than anything else. That, and sleep. If I didn't get some shut-eye soon, I was going to collapse.

Felicia wheeled her car into the parking lot of the Stumble Inn. My truck sat where I'd left it. All its vital parts seemed to still be in place. That was a relief. If we'd found it sitting up on blocks, I might've burst into tears.

"I've got to go back to the office," Felicia said.

"Don't. Come home with me. You've been working around the clock. They can spare you for a few hours."

She shook her head, which made her glasses slip down her nose.

"We're almost done. Another day with the lawyers and I might be able to finish. You go home and sleep. I'll be there as soon as I can."

I nodded and got out of the car. She leaned across the seat to look up at me.

"I'm glad you're out of jail."

"Me, too."

I bent down for a farewell kiss. While our faces were close, she said, "I love you, Bubba. Only you."

"I love you, too. Sorry I've put you through such hell."

"All in a day's work for Superwife."

She gave me a grin that I tried to return. Probably looked like I was in pain. Then I slammed the door and she peeled rubber, headed out of the parking lot.

I climbed into my trusty truck and drove toward home, trying my best to stay awake until I could reach my bed.

Twenty Nine

I'd barely gotten into my house when the phone began to ring. Against my better judgment, I answered it.

"Howdy, boy." It was Dub.

I made nice, but there wasn't much feeling in it. All I wanted was sleep.

"Took you a long time to answer the phone," he brayed. "You still in bed?"

"No, I haven't been to bed yet. I was just headed that way."

He didn't take the hint. Instead, he asked why I'd been up all night. I was too tired to concoct a lie.

"I was in jail."

"What the hell happened?"

Too late to lie now. I flopped onto the sofa and told him the whole sordid story. I didn't think I could stand to hear it again myself, but Dub was enthralled.

"So somebody shot this ole boy just as you were going out the back door?"

"Looks that way."

"Damn, that's bad timing."

"You said it."

"Sounds sort of fishy, don't it?"

"What do you mean?"

"Somebody just happens to be there at that clinic with a gun? Shoots this boy just as you're making your getaway? Sounds to me like somebody was bird-dogging you."

"What?" My mind was too foggy to track what he was saying.

"Somebody was following you. Saw you point your gun at that man. Figured now was a good time to shoot him. That way, you'd get blamed and they'd get off scot-free."

By God, he had something there. Before I could sort through it, though, he said, "Oops, gotta go. Your Mama's ready to hit the road."

"She's still with you?"

"Yep. We dropped that load and now we're headed for home."

It rankled to hear him refer to Mama's house as "home" so many years after he'd abandoned it, but I was too tired to argue.

"Where the hell are you anyway?"

"Bakersfield. That's why I was calling. To tell you we weren't coming back through Albuquerque this go-round. Your Mama's never seen the Rockies, so I'm taking her back through Colorado."

Relieved, I said that sounded like a good idea.

"Be cooler up that way, too. It's hotter than Satan's back-side here in Bakersfield."

"I'm sure."

"All right, then. I gotta go." He snickered. "Try to stay out of jail."

"Dub?"

"Yeah?"

"How about you don't mention the whole jail thing to Mama? She'll just worry."

He clucked his tongue. "Guess you're right. Too bad, too. I sure was looking forward to telling her this story."

"You've got plenty of others you can tell."

He cackled. "That's for damned sure. I'll take her up through Donner Pass, tell her about the time I hit some black ice up there—"

"Dub? Not now. I've got to go to bed."

"All right, boy. Give me a call at your Mama's in a couple of days. Let me know how this shakes out."

I pledged that I would and hung up.

Now, to bed. No more phone calls. No more fretting over the attempted murder charge. Just several hours of luxurious sleep.

I looked at a clock to calculate how much sleep I could get before Felicia was expected home from work. And then it hit me. It was nearly eleven o'clock. Melvin Haywood's flight would be setting down at the airport any minute. I exhaled loudly and got to my feet. No rest for the weary. I had a plane to meet.

Thirty

Albuquerque International Sunport is a point of pride in the city. We spent millions in taxpayer dollars to have a snazzy airport, mainly because it makes the tourists happy. It works, too. People come to the sunny Southwest and the first thing they see is the airport, all decked out in vigas and tile in "desert" colors: sand and pale pink and sky blue. Quite different from most airports, which resemble extra-large bus stations. The tourists get off the planes and ooh and aah over the Sunport. Then it's straight outside to a van that'll carry them away to trendy Santa Fe.

The Sunport is a T-shaped building with the stem of the "T" being the main concourse and the two arms holding the gates where the jets nuzzle up to the building. At the junction, there's a dramatic bronze sculpture of an Indian hoisting an eagle aloft. The huge statue leans forward, balanced on the Indian's toe, and it looks like it might topple over at any moment. Great, I always think when I see it, survive the flight only to be squished to death in the airport.

The airport was crowded with tourists in loud shirts and businessmen talking loudly into cell phones and mothers screaming loudly at romping children. I dodged them all and ran up to Haywood's gate and pressed my nose against the tall window just in time to see the blue-and-white jet roll up to the building. I was standing that way, panting for breath, when Steve Romero spoke into my ear.

"Hi, Bubba. Nice night in the cooler?"

Yipes. Enough to curl a fellow's hair.

I turned slowly and was nose to nose with my buddy, the homicide lieutenant. His square face split into a grin.

"Surprised to see me?"

I stuttered through some nonsensical answer.

"You told me your boy was out of town," he said. "Just a matter of course to check with the airlines and see whether he was flying back anytime soon. There was his name, right on the passenger list. Wednesday morning, eleven o'clock. I figured I should come down and greet him. Looks like you had the same idea."

Striving for composure, I said, "I barely made it. Felicia got me sprung this morning after my hearing. No thanks to you, I might add."

Romero grinned wider.

"You hurt my feelings, Bubba. I tried to talk Goff out of putting you on ice for the night, but he was determined. Only so much I can do."

"You know I didn't shoot Salisbury."

He shrugged his broad shoulders. "I told Goff you were too gutless to shoot somebody, but he didn't believe me."

"Thanks a lot."

People started filing out from the jetway as the plane emptied. Romero gestured to two uniformed cops I hadn't even noticed and they stationed themselves near the door. He clasped my elbow and more or less dragged me over there, too.

"We know what your client looks like," he said, "but

you can help us watch for him. We wouldn't want him slipping past."

"What are you going to do? Arrest him?"

"We've got no probable cause. Not yet, anyway. We just want to give him a ride downtown, ask him some questions."

I scanned the passengers as they unloaded, searching for Haywood. I considered trying to give him some signal that would help him escape the dragnet, but I quickly ruled it out. Romero's too sharp.

"You still think he killed Rollins?" I asked.

"I keep coming back to him and the way he split town. As Desi used to say to Lucy, he's got some 'splaining to do."

The flow of passengers began to thin. Still no sign of my client.

"Did you really not know where he was?" Romero asked.

"Would I lie to you?"

"Sure."

"I didn't know. I told him not to tell me."

"Acapulco. Flew there right after Rollins was killed. Bought the ticket on the spot, paid full price. Seems impulsive, doesn't it?"

I repeated what Haywood had told me about deciding on a vacation to mark the anniversary of his wife's cancer diagnosis.

"See, that bothers me," Romero said. "Something like that, an anniversary, a person knows that's coming up, right? Seems to me he would've booked that flight weeks ago, saved a lot of money."

"He decided to go after I told him about Rollins. He felt something had been resolved and maybe he could go off to a beach and clear his head."

"That's what he told you, huh? Better story if he iced Rollins and then hustled off to the airport to catch a plane. Makes more sense, doesn't it?"

I shrugged. Nothing made sense to me anymore.

The jetway had emptied, except for a few stragglers, those jerks who'd carried too much luggage onto the plane and now dragged it up the ramp on little click-click wheels.

I was beginning to feel queasy. I'd tried to talk Haywood out of returning to Albuquerque, but a lot had changed overnight. I was ready to see him, turn him over to Romero, get the whole thing straightened out.

"How long have you known he was in Acapulco?"

"Couple of days."

There was no point in asking why he hadn't informed me, so I instead asked, "How come you didn't go down there and get him?"

Romero chuckled. "You think my boss would let me zoom off to Acapulco on city money? We don't even have an arrest warrant for Haywood, much less enough to extradite him from Mexico. Not yet. Besides, I talked to the airline. He bought a round-trip ticket. Supposed to be getting back to town right now."

He peered down the jetway again. "Doesn't look like he's on that plane, though, does it?"

"He told me he'd be on it, that he was ready to come back and talk to you."

"Looks like he changed his mind. Maybe somebody warned him off."

"Not me."

He narrowed his eyes at me.

"Would I be here to pick him up if he wasn't coming?"

That seemed to mollify Romero. I couldn't be held responsible for what my client did as a fugitive. Well, I suppose I could, in a way. I'd told him the cops were looking for him. He'd sounded ready to face the music, but perhaps he'd decided he didn't like the tune.

"Maybe he never went to Mexico," Romero said.

"But you said—"

"I said he bought a ticket. The airline says he used it, but, hell, what do they know? He could've picked up his boarding pass, then turned right around and gone home. Or, he could've gotten off the plane in Phoenix, where he had a layover."

I winced. The truth was, a smart guy like Haywood could've faked the whole trip.

"His return flight stopped in Phoenix, too, right?" I asked.

"Yeah. He could've gotten off there. From there, he could've gone anywhere. Lot of planes in and out of Phoenix every day."

"Why didn't you have somebody watching at that airport?"

Romero rubbed his nose. "Lot to ask of our brothers in blue over in Arizona, especially since there's no charges pending. I thought he'd come back on his scheduled flight. Looks like I guessed wrong."

People had started boarding the plane for its next destination. Still no Haywood. Unless he'd hidden in the bathroom through the unloading, he hadn't been on that plane. Romero told one of the cops to go check, just in case, but we all knew it was hopeless.

Romero clapped me on the shoulder. "Cheer up. This may be good news for you. Maybe Haywood never left town. Maybe he's the one who shot Salisbury."

I remembered Dub's speculation about somebody following me to the clinic and shooting Meat. Could it have
been Haywood? Why the hell would he have done that? He
had good reason to kill Rollins, at least by some people's
standards. But I knew of no connection between him and
Mystery Meat.

Romero studied me while all this swam through my
head.

"You don't look so good, Bubba. Go home and get some
sleep."

I nodded and slumped away.

"You'll need your rest," he called from behind me.
"Goff's got big plans for you."

I turned long enough to shoot him the finger. His laughter followed me all the way up the concourse.

Thirty One

I didn't go straight home. Lovelace Medical Center isn't far from the airport, and I thought I'd stop by there, see how Ed Salisbury was doing. I bluffed my way past the front desk, got his room number, then rode the elevator up to the third floor.

The elevators opened into a hall facing the nurses' station. Interns and nurses milled around behind the counter, checking paperwork and fielding calls and putting bedpans on ice. I strolled past and counted off room numbers in search of Mystery Meat.

I worried Goff might've posted a guard outside the room as a precaution. If I spied a cop in the hall, I'd just keep walking, circle back to the elevators and get out of there. But no sign of any cops. I eased up to the wide door to Meat's room and gently pushed it open a few inches.

I didn't hear anything from inside. I figured I shouldn't loiter long, in case a nurse looked my way. I slipped inside.

The door opened into a little anteroom with a closet on one side and the bathroom on the other. I stopped there and peeked around the corner, preparing lies in case a doctor or a nurse stood at Salisbury's bedside. As soon as I could see around the corner, I yanked my head back as if shots had been fired.

Charisse Rollins sat beside the bed, holding one of Salisbury's giant paws. She wore somber clothes and she looked sleepless and worried. Salisbury was flat on his back with his eyes closed and a tube up his nose. The sheet had been pulled up to cover most of his broad, hairy chest. He was either asleep or unconscious. Either way, there wasn't much chance that I could talk to him, find out if he'd seen who shot him in the back.

Even if he'd been awake, I wouldn't have gone farther into the room. Not with Charisse sitting there. She already was steamed at me. Now she probably thought I'd shot her boyfriend. I slipped out into the hall.

A couple of nurses at the front desk eyed me as I passed, but I ignored them, too intent on making my escape. I feared Charisse might've heard me at the door, might be dashing after me. I couldn't face her.

It was a relief to make it into the elevator. I didn't waste any time getting away from the hospital.

I drove home, eager to get into bed at last. When I arrived, though, I saw the red light blinking on my answering machine. I hesitated. Whatever message awaited would delay my slumber. But maybe the message would be from Melvin Haywood, explaining why he wasn't on that plane.

"Hello, Bubba," the machine said. "This is Nancy Chilton. Call me immediately."

She sounded angry. Just what I didn't need.

Damn, I was tired of dealing with folks from The Manor. They'd worked me over every which way. They'd yelled at me, lied to me, got me mixed up in their gossip and affairs and backstabbing and murder. Got me thrown in jail. I wished I'd never met any of them.

The situation couldn't get much worse. What was one more phone call? I dialed Nancy Chilton's number.

"Well, it's about damned time," she said.

"Sorry, I've been tied up."

"I thought you were working for me."

"I was, but I spent the night in jail—"

"So I heard." —

Uh-oh.

"Boyd exploded at me last night," she said. "He's certain I hired you to follow him. I denied it, of course."

"Of course." Why should she tell the truth to her husband? That would be out of character for a resident of The Manor.

"He didn't believe me. We had a huge fight. Once he was finally asleep, I tried to call you, but you weren't there."

"Like I said, I was in jail."

"For what? Boyd wouldn't tell me."

I didn't want to go into all that again. But I gave her a brief explanation, including the standard denial that I was one who shot Ed Salisbury.

"I wouldn't blame you if you had," she said. "He's an awful man."

"So you've said."

"If you ask me, both Ed and Andrew got what they deserved."

That seemed a little extreme to me, but I said nothing. She was entitled to her opinion, even if it was skewed by her own husband's tomfoolery.

"But that's not the reason I called."

Here we go. "And that would be?"

"You're fired."

"What?"

"You're clearly incompetent. Twice I asked you to spy on my husband. Both times, it resulted in a confrontation with him. I told you I wanted this done quietly. It doesn't do me any good if he knows I'm having him followed."

"But—"

"Now the police arrest you in the Salisbury shooting. It's too much. I don't need that kind of attention. I don't want any part of it."

That gave me pause. In a way, she started all of this. It was her tip that led me to Andrew Rollins in the first place. The shit had been hitting the proverbial fan ever since. I didn't get a chance to voice that notion, however. Nancy was still talking.

"I don't expect you to return the retainer. I'll consider it the cost of a lesson well-learned. This'll be the last time I ever hire a private detective."

I'd just been thinking about how I'd like to distance myself from the denizens of The Manor, about how they'd been nothing but trouble. But it always hurts to get fired. Especially since I'd made a good effort. Things hadn't turned out well, but she didn't have to be so short with me.

I cast about for a sharp retort, something along the lines of how she'd be doing all private eyes a favor if she never hired another one, but I didn't get a chance to say it.

"Good-bye, Bubba," she snapped. "And good riddance."

I stood there with the phone against my ear until the dial tone finally began to irritate me and I hung it up.

Shit. Fired again. And my other client was missing in action. I'd gone from being flush, having two rich clients, to having none. Plus, I had an attempted murder charge and a bail bond hanging over me with "Lightning Lenny" Velasquez. Probably a buttload of legal bills to come.

I sprawled on the sofa next to the phone. Christ, I was exhausted. And sore. And pissed-off. Miserable, in a word. And it didn't look as if things were getting any better.

Thirty Two

Next thing I knew, I was awake on the sofa, my cheek damp where I'd drooled on the cushions. The phone was ringing, inches from my head. I fumbled for the receiver.

"Hello, Bubba. Melvin Haywood here."

That woke me up.

"What time is it?"

"The time? It's six o'clock. Why?"

Sunlight still slanted in through the windows. I'd only been asleep a few hours. It felt like it had been years, and that maybe midgets had beaten me with bats the whole time. My mouth was coated in moss. I smacked and coughed and tried to pull together a sentence.

"You sound funny, Bubba. Were you asleep?"

"No, no. Um, yeah. I was up all night and, wait a second, where the hell are you?"

There. I'd pulled my scattered wisps of consciousness together and remembered the pertinent question.

"Right here in Albuquerque."

"You weren't on that plane," I said accusingly.

"No, I changed my mind about the flight. I kept thinking about what you said, about the police looking for me—"

"They were at the airport! We all stood around chatting, waiting for you to get off the plane."

"Sorry about that. But it was a last-minute decision—"

"Where exactly are you right now?"

"At home. What's the matter, Bubba? You sound upset."

"Upset? Damned right I'm upset. The police are all over my ass, mostly because they can't find you."

"Oh, my, I hadn't considered that. They blame you because I didn't fly in as scheduled?"

"They didn't blame me exactly, but—"

"How did they know I was flying in today anyway? Did you tell them?"

"No, but the airline didn't mind telling them. They know you were in Acapulco. At least that's what the airline says. The cops are starting to wonder whether you ever left town."

"Of course I did. I was at the beach—"

"They think I shot Ed Salisbury!"

"Who?"

"Salisbury. Big guy? Worked with Rollins?"

"I don't know him."

"You're not going to get a chance to meet him anytime soon. He's in the hospital, after getting shot in the back yesterday."

"My goodness. And they think you did it?"

"Or you. They still think you're a good suspect for all the mayhem around here."

"But that's nonsense. I wasn't even here."

"Can you prove it?"

"Certainly. I've got receipts from the hotel—"

"I'm sure you keep careful records." He was an accountant, after all. "But they still think you're the one who clobbered Rollins. And your receipts don't give you an alibi for that, remember?"

"I thought you were working on that problem for me."

"I have been. I went back to the clinic to try to talk to Salisbury. I thought maybe he'd killed Rollins."

"Really? Do the police suspect him, too?"

"Right now, you and I are their favorites. How come you weren't on that plane?"

"I had second thoughts. I feared the police would be waiting for me, so I got off the plane in Phoenix. I've got relatives there. I borrowed a car and drove the rest of the way. I just got home a few minutes ago."

"Where did you leave the car?"

"In the garage. Why?"

"Anybody see you go in the house?"

"I don't think so. But I don't see—"

"Don't turn on the lights," I said. "Just hunker down there a while. If nobody saw you, we still have some time."

"Time for what?"

"I want to hear your whole story. See the receipts. I want you to prove to me you were really in Acapulco."

"You don't believe me?"

"Sure, I do. But we'd better have your story solid before we talk to the cops."

"They really think I killed Rollins. I can't get over that."

"You'd better find a way to believe it. We're both in a lot of trouble here, Mr. Haywood. We've got to get this straightened out."

He muttered some more, but I wasn't listening. I was trying to figure a way to meet him without bringing hordes of cops down upon us. I couldn't be sure they weren't watching his house. Or tailing me. Romero seemed to be ahead of me at every turn.

And, frankly, I wasn't sure I could trust Haywood. I still

had trouble believing Mr. Turtle could've killed anybody. But maybe he was a stellar liar. All those years fooling the IRS might've taught him to be cool under pressure. If he was the type who could lie to auditors with a straight face, how tough would it be for him to fool me?

"We need to meet someplace," I said.

"When?"

"Right away. Tonight. We need to talk."

"Why don't you come here?"

"No, I'm worried about the cops. I don't want to deal with them until we're ready."

Haywood mulled that for a minute.

"I've got an idea," he said. "Why don't we meet at the Heilbend castle?"

That confused me. Otto Heilbend's castle had been torn down generations ago.

"The foundations of the old castle are right behind my house," he said, and that cleared things up a little. "It's outside The Manor, but I can climb over my fence and meet you there. I won't have to risk driving anywhere."

"It'll have to be after dark," I said.

"How about nine o'clock?"

I agreed, and he gave me directions. A dirt road ran off into the fields just past the walls that surrounded The Manor. Follow that road to its end, he said, and I'd be at the ruins of the old castle.

"Teenagers gather out there sometimes," he said. "I've had to call the police before to break up wild parties. But there shouldn't be anyone there on a Wednesday night."

I instructed him to stay in his house with the curtains drawn until our meeting. Maybe no one had seen him arrive. Maybe he'd be safe there until nine.

I hung up the phone and fought off the urge to go back to sleep. I took a shower. Drank some coffee. Ate a sandwich. Wondered where my wife was. And, before I knew it, it was time to go meet Haywood. I hated to go unarmed, but the police still had my gun, running tests that should prove me innocent of shooting Mystery Meat.

I was nervous as hell. But I still felt it was my fault my client was suspected of murder. If there was any way to fix it, I wanted to do it. I recognized this as a noble urge, something akin to responsibility, which has never been my strong suit.

I just hoped it didn't get me killed.

Thirty Three

The road to the old Heilbend castle was deeply rutted. Summer-dry grass grew between the uneven tracks and scraped the bottom of the Ram as I eased it through the bumps, creeping along, trying not to ruin a tire. The dusty field was littered with beer bottles and malt liquor cans and similar detritus left by hard-partying teens.

The moon was a sliver—what my Mama always called Grandpa's toenail—and it didn't do much to illuminate the surroundings. Cottonwoods and wispy tamarisks clustered here and there, whispering among themselves and casting impenetrable pools of shadow. To my left, a six-foot-high concrete wall ran the length of the field, marking the perimeter of The Manor. To my right, the field stretched away into darkness.

The road ended in a spot wide enough to turn around, under the outstretched arms of a few spooky cottonwoods. I stopped the Ram and turned off the lights, but I didn't cut the engine. I wanted a chance to look around first. This seemed an odd place for a meeting with an accountant. I didn't feel any better about it the longer I sat there.

As my eyes adjusted, I could see the foundation of the old castle partly hidden in the shadows cast by the trees. Concrete and stone jutted up from the dirt a couple of feet, broken and jagged. It looked toothy, like some giant had left his lower denture lying among the weeds. The foundation stretched off twenty feet or so in either direction and backward into the darkness for God knows how far. Only one part of it had been left standing. A Gothic arch rose to a point from the center of the foundation, its stone blocks still held in place by their ancient engineering. The front door itself was long gone and the arch was covered by graffiti and blackened by the long-ago fire that had gutted the place, but the arch still stood.

No sign of Melvin Haywood. I checked the glow-in-the-dark hands on my wristwatch. Two minutes after nine. He should be here by now. I peered toward The Manor wall, half-expecting to see the little turtle-man straining to get over it. But there was no one. Finally, I shut off the truck and and got out and eased toward the foundation, clutching a heavy flashlight in my hand like a club.

I didn't switch on the light. If Haywood was hiding out here somewhere, lying in wait for me, I didn't want to make it easy for him. Better to be prepared, I told myself. You're not jumpy, you're just being careful.

I couldn't see my footing very well, and I took baby steps all the way up to the Gothic arch, feeling along, hoping not to fall into broken glass. I stepped up onto the foundation. Up here, it was still a huge floor, littered with chunks of concrete and broken tiles and the sooty remains of old bonfires.

A slight breeze riffled the dry grass and swirled the dust at my feet. It interfered with my eager listening. I strained to hear the snap of a twig, a clumsy footfall, the cocking of a hammer. My skin felt crawly and my hair was standing up like Don King's. Not a good feeling. Not the way a confident, manly private eye ought to approach a rendezvous.

Then someone said my name. I nearly jumped out of my clothes.

My head snapped around as I looked for the source of the voice. I heard it again—"Bubba!"—but I couldn't tell where it was coming from. It seemed to carry on the breeze so that it came from nowhere and everywhere. I knew it wasn't the wind. The wind cries "Mary," not "Bubba." Anybody who ever listened to Jimi Hendrix knows that.

Then the voice said, "Over here," and I got a sense it came from my left. I picked my way over the rubble of the castle foundation. As I neared the corner of the ruin, I heard a noise, a skittering in the grass, and I wheeled and flicked on my flashlight and nearly blinded Melvin Haywood.

He threw an arm up to shield his eyes and I blurted an apology and dropped the beam to his waist. He stood near a tree about fifteen feet away. He wore a dark, loose shirt, looked like maybe he'd bought it on the beach in Mexico. The type of cotton shirt that shrinks so much after one washing that you end up donating it to orphans. He also was wearing jeans and sneakers, which were out of character for Haywood, who'd seemed like such a buttoned-down guy. But the thing that really caught my attention was what he carried in his hand, down by his hip—shiny chrome-plated revolver.

I flicked out the light and scampered a few paces to my left. I tripped over a rough place on the concrete, and used the stumble as an opportunity to crouch into a squat. If Haywood planned to use that pistol, I wanted to present the smallest target possible and I wanted to keep moving. I had the high ground, still being up on the foundation, but it was a long way back to the Gothic arch. And there was no other shelter up on the concrete plain.

"Bubba!" he stage-whispered. "What are you doing?"

The flashlight had screwed up my night vision, but I was counting on it being worse for Haywood, who'd taken the beam full in the face. I duck-walked a few more feet away, trying to be quiet.

"Bubba!" Louder now. I needed to respond in some way. I didn't want him to get noisy enough to prompt a neighbor to call the cops.

I cupped my hand over my mouth, hoping to direct my voice back over to where I'd been, then said, "What are you doing with that gun?"

I could see Haywood in silhouette, his shape black against the lighter, dusty ground beyond. He cast the palest of moon shadows. He raised the hand that held the pistol and I flinched, but then I got the idea that he'd sort of forgotten he'd brought the gun with him.

"This?" Like I could've meant some other gun out here in the middle of freaking nowhere.

"Drop it," I said, trying to sound like Gary Cooper.

"Come on, Bubba. I just brought this along for protection. It's dark out here and—"

"Put it down."

He tilted his head to one side like he was thinking it over. I still counted on him not being able to see me, but that wouldn't last much longer. And once he spotted me, he'd see I wasn't carrying a gun, that my demands were a big bluff.

Then he bent at the waist and set the pistol on the ground by his feet. I exhaled with relief, so vigorously that it made my nose whistle.

I turned the flashlight on again, aimed it at Haywood's chest, and approached.

"What are you so anxious about?" he asked. "Did you think I planned to shoot you?"

"No," I lied, then added: "Way things have been going lately, you can't be too careful. Somebody shot Ed Salisbury, remember?"

He didn't show any reaction to that. I thought I'd loaded it with meaning. The fact that Haywood owned a handgun seemed to make him a better suspect in the Salisbury shooting. But he didn't seem to get it.

"Can I pick up my gun now?" he asked.

"What for?"

"It's going to get all dirty."

"Just take a couple of steps back," I said. "I'll take care of it."

He did as he was told. I leaped down off the castle foundation and bent over to pick up the gun. Just in time I thought about fingerprints—what if this turned out to be the gun that shot Mystery Meat?—and grasped it by the very tip of its barrel. I turned and set the gun on the edge of the concrete footing, where he'd have to go through me to get it.

"Okay," I said. "We've got some talking to do."

I switched off the flashlight and let darkness envelop us. I looked over toward The Manor, but nobody seemed to be watching. The flashlight and our voices hadn't alerted anyone or set any dogs to barking. Maybe the folks over there were so accustomed to teenaged orgies, they didn't even notice a couple of guys slipping around in the dark.

"I've already told you everything I know. I swear to you, I didn't harm anyone."

He sounded so sincere, I let my guard down a little. I reminded myself this guy was my client. And gun or no gun, it was hard to believe mild Melvin might've killed.

"I believe you," I said, trying to sound convincing. "But

cops aren't so trusting. We have to cook up something that will make them believe you're innocent."

So we stood there in the dark, chatting. He told me again how he'd gotten the wild idea about taking a vacation on the morning Rollins was killed. He'd packed a bag and gone to the airport to buy his ticket. The jet to Acapulco had seats available and he'd purchased one with a credit card. Then, while waiting for his flight to be called, he'd phoned his office to tell them he'd be out of town.

"I didn't tell them where I was going or how they could reach me," he said. "At the time, it seemed that would have defeated the whole purpose of my little getaway."

"Don't say 'getaway' when you talk to the cops," I interrupted.

"Oh, yes. Right you are. Anyhow, I boarded the plane and flew to Phoenix, where I changed planes."

"You talk to anybody on those flights? See anybody you knew?"

"No. In fact, I napped most of the way. It felt like the first good sleep I'd had in the past year."

"What about the flight attendants? People at the airport?"

"I can't imagine any of them would remember me."

I had to agree. He was such a gray little man, he was practically invisible.

"What about at the hotel?"

"Certainly. I talked to the manager there. A very nice fellow named Sanchez. He'd remember me. And maybe some of the waiters would, too."

Great, I'm thinking, his alibi hinges on Mexican waiters.

"They certainly could vouch for me being there when this Salisbury person was shot," he said. "But I'm afraid that doesn't help with the Rollins murder."

I hitched up my jeans and stared into the darkness.

"I thought Salisbury killed Rollins," I said, "but him getting shot screwed that up. It would seem logical that whoever killed Rollins was the same one who wounded Salisbury. At least, that's the way the cops are treating it."

We both mulled that awhile.

"Perhaps," Haywood offered, "Salisbury did kill Rollins and then somebody found out he'd done it and tried to get even."

"You mean somebody wanted to avenge the doctor's death?"

I hadn't run across anybody who'd seemed that loyal to Rollins. The guy appeared to be roundly despised. The only person who might've cared enough to seek revenge—his wife—had been shtupping Salisbury on the side.

"I don't know," I said. "Doesn't make sense to me."

"Maybe it's an avenue you can pursue."

Pursue? He still wanted me on the case? I was surprised. I'd figured we'd do the best we could, getting his story straight, then I'd hand him over to the cops and let them sort it out. I said something to that effect and he said, "No, no, that won't do. I trust you, Bubba. I don't think I can expect fair treatment from the police. They're too intent on solving the murder. They won't believe me."

What could I say? He was right. Romero and friends just wanted to do their jobs and move on to the next case. Why would they give Haywood the benefit of the doubt?

"Here," he said, "I have something for you."

He reached into the pocket of his shirt. I braced myself in case he came up with another weapon, but it was a slip of paper. He handed it over. It was the size and shape of my favorite type of paper—a check.

I turned the flashlight on long enough to look at the

amount. A thousand dollars. I turned the light off.

"That may not seem like much," he said, though it seemed like plenty to me, "but I know you've gone through a lot for me already. I want you to stay on the case. Figure out who killed Rollins. Then I'll be ready to talk to the police."

If he was trying to buy my loyalty, a thousand bucks was a pretty good start. Besides, it wasn't like I could drop the case now. I was in too deep.

"Okay, I'll keep after it," I said. "You lie low for a day or two. Just stay in your house, keep the lights off, don't let anybody see you. Maybe we can buy enough time for me to sort this out. I keep feeling like I'm right on top of a solution."

Then flashlight beams shot through the night from several directions, all aimed at us. I was blinded for a second, but I sensed Haywood move past me quickly. As I turned toward him, I saw him snatch up the pistol from where I'd left it on the concrete slab. He wheeled around, blinking against the lights.

"Police! Drop that weapon!"

Haywood looked confused. He swiveled around, pointing the gun at everything, at nothing. Yikes. I reached out and clipped him on the wrist with my flashlight, hard enough that he dropped the pistol in the dirt. Then I backed away, expecting bullets to come flying.

"Hands up!" the cop voice said. "Show us your hands!"

My hands went up so fast, they nearly lifted me off the ground. Haywood was holding the wrist I'd hit against his chest.

"Do it, Melvin," I said. "I don't want to die out here."

Haywood lifted his arms into the air. He hung his head. And then they were upon us.

Thirty Four

Dark-uniformed cops spun Haywood and me around and threw us against the concrete foundation and frisked us. Melvin grunted objections to the rough handling, but I kept quiet. The way he'd swung that gun around, we were lucky to be alive.

The cops cuffed our hands behind our backs and hoisted us to our feet.

Flashlight beams danced crazily in the darkness, and I couldn't make out much, but I could see the one person I needed to see: Lieutenant Steve Romero, rocking on his heels ten feet away, his grin glowing in the night.

"Hey, Bubba," he said. "Nice evening, huh?"

"What the hell—"

"Imagine my surprise to find you out here, chit-chatting with Mr. Haywood. I thought you didn't know where he was."

"He called me this afternoon. We were making plans for his surrender."

"Funny, that's not what I heard. I heard him trying to buy you off."

Romero came close and dipped a hand in my hip pocket and pulled out Haywood's check. He held it under his flashlight and whistled when he saw the amount.

"Damn," he said, "you work cheap, don't you?"

That didn't seem to merit a reply. I had more pressing matters to discuss. "What are you doing out here in the middle of the night?"

Romero ignored me. He ordered a couple of the uniforms to go fetch patrol cars, which they'd apparently left parked along Rio Grande Boulevard. Certainly no cars had come bumping down the dirt road while Haywood and I were there. Romero had five or six uniformed cops hustling around in the dark. How had I not noticed them? And how much of my conversation with Haywood had they heard?

"Got a telephone tip down at headquarters tonight," Romero said. "Some lady called Homicide and said your buddy Melvin here had just climbed over the wall behind his house and was headed toward this old ruin."

I glanced over at Haywood. His head hung down until his chin practically touched his chest. He didn't move. Once again, he acted the turtle. Just tucked in his head and waited for it all to be over.

"A woman?" I asked. "Who was she?"

"She didn't leave a name. But the sergeant who took the call knew I'd been hunting your friend here and he called me at home. I used the radio to get some uniforms over here, told them to tiptoe. You guys stood around blabbing so long, we had time to sneak right up to you."

"I never heard a thing."

"We cops can be stealthy when we need to."

"Like when you're sneaking up on a doughnut?"

One of the uniforms jabbed me in the back. Romero shook his head at him and smiled at me.

"Go ahead, Bubba. Mouth off all you want. Maybe it'll make you feel better."

"I doubt it."

One of the uniforms grabbed my elbow and led me away a few paces. Another did the same to Haywood. I didn't know what they were up to at first, but then I saw them bagging Haywood's fallen pistol.

"If you were listening," I said to Romero, "then you know Haywood was out of town when Salisbury was shot."

"So he says."

"He's got documents from the hotel." I sounded desperate in my own ears.

"We'd love to see 'em. He's going to have lots of time to persuade me he really was in Mexico. I expect Melvin and I will be talking all night."

Haywood loosed a little groan.

Cop cars came bumping up the dirt track, moving too fast, their headlights bouncing jerkily. The uniforms stood around grinning. They seemed to be enjoying themselves, out arresting people on a breezy summer night. Their idea of a good time. And me? I felt like I'd stumbled into the wrong party.

"I can see that you need to talk to Mr. Haywood," I said. "We were going to come in and see you. Really. But why am I cuffed?"

Romero used the flashlight to scratch his wide chin. The light shone up his face, throwing shadows, giving him a creepy countenance.

"How about harboring a fugitive?"

"I wasn't harboring him. I met him here. I tried to convince him to turn himself in."

"That's not what I heard. I believe your exact words were 'lie low for a day or two.'"

Oops.

"That was part of my plan to get him to surrender," I said lamely.

"Some plan."

Another car jolted toward us on the dirt road. I couldn't make out its details, but I could see it didn't have red lights on the top.

A couple of the cops tucked Haywood into the back of a squad car. I figured I was next. I couldn't face another night in jail. And I dreaded the thought of Felicia having to bail me out again. Assuming I could get bail. A judge wouldn't look kindly on me being arrested two days in a row.

A car door slammed and I swiveled my head to look over at the most recent arrival. From the glow of headlights, I could make out the figure of Sgt. Irwin Goff headed our way. Shit.

Goff's shaved head shone in the half-light as he said to Romero, "The office told me I'd find you here." He took him aside and they muttered in low tones. I strained to hear, expecting any second for the uniforms to haul me away.

Instead, once the conversation ended, they both approached and Romero told the cop nearest me, "Take the cuffs off him."

I felt a seed of hope sprout within me. "What's up?"

"You just got a lucky break, Bubba," Romero said.

The cop got the cuffs off and I rubbed at my wrists, trying to get the blood flowing.

"Ed Salisbury finally came to," Goff intoned. "He says you didn't fire the shot."

"He did?" I was stunned.

"He hated to admit it," Goff said. "Seems he doesn't like you much. But he said you'd gone out the door when the bullet hit him in the back. Somebody else fired that shot. He didn't see who pulled the trigger, but he says it wasn't you."

Romero pointed his flashlight toward the car where Haywood sat in the back seat, looking miserable.

"We took a gun off Haywood. We'll test it. There's still a chance he's your shooter."

"Mabry's gun came up clean," Goff said, glaring at me. I could tell my sudden innocence had ruined his evening. I tried to keep from smiling.

"So you're dropping the attempted murder charge?" I asked.

"Seems I don't have any choice," Goff said. "We can file it again if I find out Salisbury is wrong about you."

"Well, then," I said, "looks like I've got a pretty good case for false arrest."

Goff growled something under his breath, but Romero cut in before he could take out his frustrations on my head.

"Don't push it, Bubba. There's still plenty of charges we could bring. Assault with a deadly weapon, for instance. Abetting a fugitive."

Gulp.

"Just kidding. The arrest was an honest mistake."

Goff turned on his heel and marched off toward his car, muttering.

"You had to tweak him, didn't you, Bubba?"

"Sorry. Couldn't help myself."

"Yeah? Well, don't be surprised if he really does file charges against you. Goff's not a man you want to mess with."

He was right, of course. I kept contritely silent while Romero looked me over.

"All right," he said to the uniforms after a moment,

"let's take Haywood downtown."

"What about me?" I asked.

"You're free to go. For now."

"Shouldn't I come down to the station? Maybe I should be there when you question Haywood."

"You his lawyer now? I didn't know you'd passed the bar."

"Okay, I'll go home."

"Good idea. Get some rest. You look like hell."

"So I hear."

Romero clapped me on the shoulder with one of his big hands. Which smarted. Then he and the others piled into the squad cars and bumped away. Haywood's silhouette in the back seat looked pitiful and small. He didn't even turn to look at me as they hauled him away.

And I felt even worse.

Thirty Five

Felicia was sound asleep when I got home, which was just as well. I was too despondent and exhausted to explain where I'd been and how I'd failed my client. I undressed in the dark and crawled into bed beside her, figuring I'd be awake for hours, reliving everything I'd done wrong. But within seconds, it seemed, I was out cold.

Felicia lay in wait for me when I awoke late the next morning. I heard her crashing around in the kitchen. I didn't feel ready to face her, but I desperately needed coffee.

She was still in her bathrobe, chatty and chipper, glad to finally be done with her big investigative project. I slurped coffee and let her chatter, too distressed to take pleasure in her return to our home.

"So what's the matter with you?" she asked finally. "Something happen last night? You were pretty late."

No use trying to evade. It only makes Felicia more dogged. I told her, in the tersest possible terms, about Haywood's arrest. The only bright spot in the whole mess was Goff dropping the attempted murder charges against me.

"That's great news, Bubba," she said. "We can get the bond lifted."

"Don't be too hasty," I said glumly. "Goff seems eager to

charge me with something else. You might want to keep Lightning Lenny's phone number handy."

I explained about the possibility of an assault charge or a harboring beef, but she shook me off.

"I'd take either of those over attempted murder, any day."

I had to admit she was right. At least I wasn't in custody, which was more than I could say for Melvin Haywood.

I guess I was frowning because Felicia said, "Now what?"

"Just thinking about Haywood. I assume they questioned him all night. And the worst isn't over. Good chance his reputation will be ruined, whether he did it or not."

She shook her head. "All because he was so jealous."

"I should've never told him about Rollins. Maybe none of this would've happened."

Felicia got up to refill our coffee cups.

"Tell me again," she said. "How did you even find out it was Rollins?"

"Nancy Chilton told me. She's the neighborhood busy-body."

"Wonder if she's the one who ratted you out to the cops last night? Can you see Haywood's house from where she lives? Maybe she spotted him climbing over that wall."

"I wouldn't put it past her. She wouldn't pass up a chance to meddle in other people's business. And she's still pretty mad at me."

Felicia grinned and pushed up her glasses.

"She's about to have more reasons to be pissed off," she said.

"How's that?"

"We nailed her husband. Boyd Chilton's been moving

hot cars, just like the rest of those assholes. It'll all be in the paper tomorrow."

That made me feel better. I still bore a grudge against Chilton over my ruined camera and the scene at the Stumble Inn. I'd be happy to see him make some headlines, and I told Felicia so.

"He probably won't be the lead story," she said. "Apparently, he's only recently dipped into the scam. Some of the others have been moving stolen cars and doing odometer rollbacks and other crap for years. Somebody buys a car—low mileage, new paint, seems fine—only to find out later it's a disguised lemon, or that it was stolen in someplace like St. Louis and given a new life out here."

"Sounds like you and Jake are going to make waves with this one."

She harrumphed. "Jake will get second billing on the byline, and he's lucky to get that. I wrote nearly the entire package while he was off playing detective, tailing these dealers. But he'll find a way to take the credit if these bozos end up going to jail."

Now my grin was genuine. "Sounds like you've soured on old Jake."

"What can I say? He's a TV type. I hear he's already sniffing around the local stations, trying to relocate. Good riddance, I'd say. I'm tired of being his producer, doing all the work so he can look good."

I don't know why this improved my mood so much. I'd already received Felicia's assurances that there was nothing between her and Jake. And I'd believed her. Really. But to hear her bad-mouth him made me feel much better somehow.

I got out of my chair and went around the table and gave

her a big hug. When I broke the clench, she looked puzzled, but happy.

"I'm glad to have you home again," I said. "Don't take on any more big projects for a while. All these long hours are bad for us. I miss you too much."

She flushed and smiled and tilted up her face to be kissed. I obliged her, but I was thinking how I'd been a fool to act so jealous and weird before. I'd become infected by the denizens of The Manor, all of them sleeping around like rabbits. Andrew and Charisse and Mystery Meat and the Chiltons. Poor old Melvin Haywood and his undying love for his dead wife, who'd cheated on him.

And then something hit me. I sputtered in Felicia's face. She leaned away from me, giving me a look like I was a head case.

"I just thought of something," I said, my mind whirring. "I've got to go."

I raced into the bedroom and threw on some clothes. Felicia trailed me to the front door, looking bewildered. I blew her a kiss as I ran for my truck.

Thirty Six

Sometimes, inspiration comes from the strangest places. Maybe it was the electrical charge I got from kissing my sweetie. Maybe it was the names of all The Manor residents tripping through my head. All I know is that something clicked. I realized I'd skipped over something, and it might be the key.

What flashed in my mind was the sign-in sheet at the front desk at the Rollins clinic. Romero had told me no one could put Charisse or Haywood in the clinic when Rollins was killed. I'd successfully sneaked in past the front desk the day Salisbury was shot, but I couldn't imagine Nurse Wyborn let that happen often. If Dub was right and somebody had been following me that day, maybe they signed that log to get inside. It was a long shot, but if a name on the log matched up with any of the names from the day Rollins was clubbed to death . . .

I drove like a madman over to the clinic. I didn't know whether Nurse Wyborn would be willing to help me. And she was burly enough that she could probably toss me outside the way Meat had. But I had to risk it. I had to get a look at those logs.

Dark clouds bulked up on the western horizon, teasing us with the prospect of a monsoon. The wind blew grit across Lomas as I reached the clinic. I prayed the clouds would let loose and wash the city clean.

I jerked the Ram into a parking slot and hurried into the waiting room. Only a couple of patients flipping through magazines.

Nurse Hildegarde Wyborn filled the little window into the reception office. She scowled when she saw me. Her hand went to a phone, and I guessed she was ready to dial 911.

"Hold on there," I said. "I'm not here to cause trouble."

Her hand didn't leave the phone, but she didn't pick up the receiver either. I took a deep breath and began.

"Everybody who comes in here signs that log, right?" I pointed to the clipboard on the counter between us.

Her big head moved an inch. I took it to be a nod.

"Do you keep those logs? File them somewhere?"

Another nod.

"Can I get a look at them? I'm thinking that whoever's been attacking people around here maybe signed in."

"The police already looked at the sign-in sheets. They questioned our patients."

"But did they look at them after Salisbury was shot? Try to match them up?"

She had to admit she didn't know. It seemed to pain her. I, on the other hand, was tickled to death. I figured Goff and Romero hadn't compared notes on the two incidents at the clinic. One a murder, the other an assault, the cases went to different divisions of the APD. And Romero and Goff didn't seem to like each other much. Probably the less they talked, the better both liked it.

"May I see the logs?" I asked Nurse Wyborn. "Please?"

She shook her head and her saggy jowls trembled.

"Private records," she said. "I'd need authorization."

"Who's going to give it to you?" I lowered my voice so the waiting patients couldn't hear. "Rollins is dead. Salisbury's in the hospital. Who's in charge?"

She didn't seem willing to answer that question, but I knew the answer. No one was in charge. I was dealing with a rudderless ship here. The clinic was drifting along until somebody—Charisse? Salisbury?—could turn it into a money-maker again. Without a boss to make the decision, Nurse Wyborn didn't know which way to jump. And her philosophy seemed to be: Better to refuse than to get in trouble later.

"Okay, look," I said in exasperation. "Could you at least look at those logs? Maybe you'll notice the same name crops up on both of them."

She hesitated. I needed something else to sway her.

"It might help me find Dr. Rollins' killer," I said, counting on her loyalty to her dead boss. "We don't want the killer getting away with it, do we?"

She thought it over some more, and I was already calculating how to get Romero to show up with a warrant, when she said, "I suppose that wouldn't hurt anything. Go through that door over there and come into this office. You're disturbing the waiting room."

I was a little uneasy about being in close quarters with a sumo wrestler like Nurse Wyborn, but I did as I was told. I went through the door into the hallway, then hung a hard left through the door of the reception office. She pulled open one of the filing cabinets that lined the wall and produced a folder stuffed full of white paper.

"These are all the logs for the past three months," she said. "We don't keep them any longer than that. Sometimes, patients can't remember when they were last in the clinic. We keep these handy so we don't have to go dig out their records."

I nodded along, trying not to let my eagerness show.

She rifled through the pages until she found the right ones. She held the sheets side by side, letting her eyes roam the names. It was all I could do not to snatch them out of her hands. I caught myself trying to go up on tiptoe to see over the tops of the pages, and tried to relax. I was getting what I wanted, as long as I didn't rush her.

A minute passed before she said, "Too bad about your theory, Sherlock. None of the names match."

"There's no duplication? No one signed in on both of those days?"

She shook her head. "Not a one."

Damn. I felt like I'd been gut-punched. I'd really thought I was onto something. Proof that the same person had been in the clinic at the times of both incidents would've at least been a start toward a solution. Of course, it was possible the shooter had slipped past the front desk without signing the sheet. If a galoot like me could get away with that, surely someone intent on murder could've accomplished it. Or, the shooter could've put down a fake name. Or, maybe it was somebody who worked at the clinic and already was there every day without signing in at all.

I gave Nurse Wyborn the hard eye, wondering whether she had any reason to kill Rollins, but she didn't notice. She still studied the sign-up sheets.

"That's odd," she said.

"What?"

She ran her eyes up and down the sheets once more before answering.

"I distinctly remember one of our patients being here at the clinic the day Mr. Salisbury was injured. I saw her in the hall when I went to call the police because of you and your stupid gun. But her name's not on the list anywhere. I wonder why she didn't sign in?"

I had a pretty good idea why.

"Was she here the day Dr. Rollins was killed?"

"I seem to remember seeing her . . . "

My heart thumped as I asked the next, most important question, "Can you tell me who it is?"

Nurse Wyborn frowned at the sign-in sheets. I was practically dancing with impatience.

"I suppose so," she said. "If you think it'll help."

"Oh, it'll help. Believe me. Just tell me the name."

Thirty Seven

The Ram's tires screeched as I reined it to a stop in front of Nancy Chilton's massive home. I wasn't worried about the noise. If I was right, everyone in The Manor would be hearing about Nancy Chilton soon.

The clouds had rushed into position over the city, and hot wind snatched at my hair as I hurried up the sidewalk to her front door. Thunder rumbled with anticipation as I rang the doorbell.

It took Nancy a minute to answer the bell. Thunder boomed again, and the first fat raindrops hit the ground. The air filled with desert perfume, that musty, sweet fragrance of water in a dry place.

I breathed deeply, trying to get my excitement under control. I needed to be outwardly calm. My goal was to make Nancy talk, not to scare her away. I couldn't hold a gun on her the way I had with Mystery Meat. (I didn't even have a gun. The cops still had it.) I needed to make her think I'm on her side, get her to tell me exactly what happened.

A wind gust blew rain my way and drops freckled my shirt. I was reaching for the doorbell again when Nancy opened the door.

She seemed surprised to see me. She'd probably figured that firing me had gotten rid of me forever. She didn't let my appearance at her door ruffle her, though. She looked cool and well-tended, wearing black flats and black slacks and a starched peach-colored blouse. She'd turned up the collar on the blouse so it framed her handsome face.

"What do you want?" she said by way of greeting.

"We need to talk."

I pushed past her before she could slam the door. She followed me into the living room. A ray of sunlight had eluded the clouds outside and poured through the tall windows, casting buttery pools on the fat furniture. I flung myself into a sunlit armchair, crossed my legs and tried to look nonchalant.

Nancy seemed perturbed, but she didn't order me out of her house. She stepped around the coffee table and sat on a sofa across from me. She opened the antique wooden box on the table and pulled out a brown cigarette and lit it. Then she leaned back and blew smoke out her nose and studied me, waiting.

Somebody stares at me too long, I start getting jittery. Try it on your dog sometime. They don't like it. And neither do I.

Thunder roared again, and closing clouds switched off the sunbeam. The rainfall picked up another notch, hammering on the roof, spattering the tall windows until the view was muddled. It made the room feel smaller, and Nancy shifted on the couch, still waiting me out.

"You lied to me," I said flatly.

Her eyebrows arched, but still she said nothing.

"Andrew Rollins never had an affair with Eileen Haywood, did he?"

A smile tugged at her lips, and I knew I had her. She thought that lie was the only reason I was here. But I had much more.

"All right," she said finally. "That wasn't exactly the truth. Eileen did have an affair, but it wasn't with Andrew. It was a quick fling with a pool boy. Years ago. She told me about it because she still felt guilty. I told her to keep it to herself, but I guess it got to her when she was on her deathbed."

I filed away the mention of the "pool boy." I could use that later.

"In fact," I said, leaning forward in my eagerness, "you were the one who had an affair with Andrew Rollins, weren't you?"

Her eyebrows shot up. It took her a second to collect herself, but then she said, "Are you insane?"

"No more lies," I said sternly. "That was the case, wasn't it? You and Andrew?"

She tapped her cigarette against the edge of a ceramic ashtray. She looked ready to laugh in my face.

"I wouldn't have touched Andrew Rollins with a redwood tree," she said. "He was a womanizing snake. And he was a fool, letting Ed and Charisse carry on right under his nose. I tried to tell him they were making an ass out of him, but he wouldn't listen."

Okay, so I'd been wrong about Nancy and Rollins. It took me a second to regroup.

"You told him this when?" I asked. "The day he died?"

"Very good, Bubba," she said condescendingly. "You might've finally figured something out."

I didn't like her tone. The thunder boomed again, and it prompted me to rush my next question.

"You hit him with that dumbbell, didn't you?"

She took another long drag on the cigarette, eyeing me through a cloud of smoke.

"I think you'd better leave now," she said. "I don't want to talk to you anymore."

I leaped to my feet. My face felt hot. My fists were clenched beside my thighs. Where did she get off, thinking she could just dismiss me, when I had the goods on her?

"Oh, you'll talk all right," I said. "You love to talk. Your whole life revolves around talking, talking, talking. Gossiping about your neighbors. Telling lies to me."

She tried to keep her cool, but I could see in her eyes that she was afraid I might spring at her, take out my frustrations on her with my fists. I certainly planned nothing of the kind, but I wasn't completely in control of myself anymore, either.

You want somebody to talk, you've got to hit them where it hurts.

I stood up and crossed to the stone fireplace. Nancy's prized Pueblo pottery sat on the mantel, looking fat and shiny. Track lighting set into the ceiling illuminated each of her treasures. I picked up one of the pots, a black one with white designs etched into it. I pretended to study it for a moment, then I looked up at Nancy and our eyes met. I gave her a little grin and let the pot drop from my hands.

She shrieked. Thunder cracked as the pot shattered on the hearth.

Nancy tensed all over as if to jump up from the couch, but she caught herself and sat still. She took a nervous drag off her cigarette, watching me carefully.

I leaned against the mantel, let my arm lie along its cool length.

"Why did you tell me Eileen Haywood had slept with Rollins?"

"I just wanted to stir the pot a little," she said.

"Don't say 'pot.'" I blithely pushed another pot to its doom. Nancy jumped as it crashed to the floor.

I slid along the mantel, rested my hand on the next pot.

"That one's worth a fortune," she said.

"Oopsy-daisy." Crash.

I picked up the next pot in line, held it out toward her. "You ready to talk now?"

"I was upset about Ed and Charisse," she said stiffly. "I thought that maybe, if you started asking questions, Rollins might put his own house in order."

Things began to click into place inside my head.

"So it wasn't Rollins you were after. It was Salisbury."

She closed her eyes and exhaled smoke toward the ceiling. She shrugged, as if she'd lost an argument with herself.

"Ed and I had been seeing each other for months," she said. "I was falling in love with him. Then he scampered off after Charisse. Men. Always going for younger women."

She stubbed out the cigarette and crossed her arms under her breasts. She looked as if she was holding herself together.

"Then you showed up on my doorstep, asking about Eileen Haywood. I don't know why I told you she'd had an affair with Andrew. It was an impulse. I was so upset about Ed. I just wanted him back."

"But it didn't work," I said.

She shook her head. She wasn't looking at me anymore. She stared at a watercolor on the opposite wall. Wild horses running free across a prairie. I wondered what the painting meant to her, and if she knew her days of running free were running short.

"It was a sort of game, siccing you on Andrew," she said. "I followed you to the clinic, watched Ed throw you out of the place. I could see you weren't going to get anywhere."

That stung, but I said nothing.

"So I went back there the next morning myself," she continued. "I breezed right in, acting like I belonged there, and I found Andrew alone in that workout room. I tried to talk some sense into him, tried to get him to do something about Charisse and the way she'd lured Ed away from me. But he just laughed me off. He didn't care what she did. He probably was already on the lookout for Wife Number Four."

The rain began to let up outside. Soon the clouds would blow through, on their collision course with the Sandia Mountains. The rain quickly would become a memory. And the whole city would start holding its breath again, waiting for the next monsoon.

When I spoke, my voice was low. "Rollins made you angry."

She took a deep breath and looked away, breaking the spell she'd been under. I thought she'd refuse to say more, but she couldn't stop talking now that she'd come this far.

"Yes, he made me angry. He said unkind things about how Charisse was more desirable than me. He dismissed me as a hysterical woman. So I picked up a dumbbell that was sitting right there and I swung it at him."

"And it killed him."

"I didn't mean to do that. I just lashed out in anger and, the next thing I knew, he was lying there on the floor with his skull bashed in. I wiped the dumbbell off with a towel and got out of there."

On rubbery legs, I carried the pottery back to my chair. I needed to sit down.

I'd come here to get a confession out of Nancy Chilton,

but some part of me hadn't expected to succeed. Now that she'd told me her secrets, I felt sort of dizzy, as if the horizons of my world had been tilted.

"You got away with it," I said finally. "So why did you hire me?"

"To keep an eye on you. You were poking around, trying to prove poor Melvin had nothing to do with Andrew's death. I was afraid you'd stumble onto something that would implicate me. I thought I could steer you, sic you on Ed. I guess I thought that, if you and the police were watching him, he'd stay away from Charisse. But I was wrong. He practically moved in with her right away. That hurt."

Her eyes were wet, but she struggled against the tears and took a deep, shuddering breath.

"You never cared that your husband was running around on you?"

She shook her head and tried to smile through the tears.

"Boyd's been having affairs for years. I've got the life I wanted when I married him. We're well off. He has his little flings and I have mine. None of it means anything."

"But you fell for Salisbury."

She hesitated. "I wanted him back. I was jealous. Plotting and scheming the whole time, when I should've seen it was too late. The clinic, everything Andrew built up, could be Ed's as long as he kept Charisse happy. He'd see that. He's that kind of guy."

We sat in silence while she composed herself. I had another round of questions to ask, then I 'd call the cops.

"You tailed me, while I was working for you?"

"Off and on. It's pretty easy to follow you around. You drive that big red truck. I wanted to see what you were doing, see if it was making any difference. But you kept screwing up."

I winced. Unfortunately, she was right.

"Then you went hustling over to the clinic that morning to talk to Ed. I saw how you walked right in without seeing the nurse. I peeked into the hall just as you went into the exercise room where Andrew died. That worried me. I followed and listened at the door and I could hear you talking to Ed, but I couldn't make out what you were saying. I was afraid Ed was telling you about me. Then that fat nurse came waddling down the hall. I walked past her, as if I was leaving. When she ran past me to her office, I went back to the gym. I saw you going out the back door with a gun in your hand."

"And you saw your opportunity. You could shoot Salisbury and it would look like I'd done it."

She pressed her lips tightly together. She'd admitted a lot already, but she didn't seem willing to say that she'd set me up, not with me sitting right there.

"You've got nothing else to say?" I asked after a while.

"I wish my aim had been better."

I got up from my chair. A phone sat on an end table near the sofa. I walked over to it, keeping my distance from Nancy Chilton. I set the pot on the table beside the phone and dialed the number for Homicide. When a man answered, I asked for Romero. He said Romero wasn't there.

"I need to reach him. I've got a murder suspect for him."

Nancy wasn't looking at me. She casually leaned forward and opened the antique box on the coffee table for another cigarette.

The detective who'd answered the phone put me on hold and I turned toward Nancy, just in time to see her pull a small, flat pistol from the box.

"Hang up the phone," she said. I did as I was told.

She stood and moved away from me, keeping the gun pointed at my navel. I had a burning sensation in my gut, as if I could anticipate the bullet's pathway.

"Put the gun down. You don't want to get into worse trouble."

Her smile was hideous.

"How could it get any worse? You're a loose end, Bubba. Time to get rid of you."

I saw her finger tighten on the trigger and I scooped up the Indian pot and hurled it at her. It was a lucky shot, but the pot hit her gun hand. The gun went off, blowing a fuzzy chunk out of the back of the armchair.

I lunged forward, diving through the air as the gun went pow-pow-pow behind me. I landed on the hard tile floor, a Navajo rug scrunched up under my hip. Then I rolled, trying to get the fat armchair between me and the gun.

The gun cracked twice more, but luckily Nancy Chilton's aim *was* pretty lousy. Splinters flew off an antique table beside the chair. A vase exploded near my head.

I jumped up and ran for the front door. The framed watercolor of the running horses shattered by my head, showering glass everywhere. I hit the deck again, frantically crawling around the floor, trying to find a hidey-hole.

Nancy stalked toward me, the gun aimed at my head. I was on all fours, flinching against the bullet I expected in my brain any second. She stumbled a little as she stepped onto the wadded-up Navajo rug. She threw up her hands to keep her balance and I snatched the edge of the rug, yanking it out from under her.

Nancy's feet shot out from under her and she fell onto her back. The breath was knocked out of her, but she swung the little peashooter my way too quickly for me to make a grab for it. Besides, I was busy scurrying for cover.

The front door crashed open and Romero and a troop of uniformed cops came charging through. Their clothes were peppered with raindrops and they all had weapons drawn. Never have I been so happy to see policemen.

Romero leveled his pistol at Nancy and said, "Drop that gun. Do it now."

I crouched behind a chair. I heard her gun hit the tiles and I peeked over the back of the chair to see her sitting on the floor, her face flushed, her hands empty.

I stood up, brushed at the knees of my jeans and tucked at my shirttail, trying to act like I wasn't bothered by a woman popping off several rounds at me within the confines of a living room. Once Nancy was cuffed, I turned to Romero.

"How did you know I was here?"

"A nurse called the office. A Ms. Wyborn?"

I nodded.

"She said you'd come by to look at those sign-in logs at the clinic and that she'd told you about Mrs. Chilton being on the premises the day Salisbury was shot. She said you went racing out of there. I figured you'd come over here."

"Thought you'd come to my rescue?"

"Didn't know you'd need rescuing. You were already inside when we rolled up. I saw your truck and told the guys to wait a few minutes, see what happened. Then we heard shots and I knew it was time to pull your fat out of the fire."

Damn. I'd come so close to pulling this off on my own.

"I got a complete confession out of her," I said, grasping at what success I'd managed. "I was calling you when she pulled that gun on me."

"She shot Salisbury?"

"Yep. Killed Rollins, too."

Nancy finally had zipped her lips. She glowered at me as Romero asked, "How'd you get her to confess?"

I pointed to the shards on the hearth. "I killed some pottery."

Nancy sounded like she was choking. The uniforms led her out to the squad cars. She glared at me over her shoulder as she went through the front door.

Romero squinted at me. "Looks like she's done talking. You got any proof?"

"I'm guessing that gun on the floor was the one that shot Salisbury. For starters. And we can place her at the clinic when Rollins was killed."

Romero scratched at his chin, pondering.

"But why, Bubba? Why'd she do it?"

"For love."

"Love?"

"Crazy, huh?"

Epilogue

I t took months, of course, and much nervous testimony from me, but Nancy Chilton was convicted of first-degree murder and sentenced to life in the state women's prison. She took the sentencing without tears or complaint. She had only one thing to say to the bench: "I'll be happy to spend the rest of my life in a place where there are no men."

Ed Salisbury blew out a knee while undergoing physical therapy following his hospital stay. He had a splint on his leg, but he and Charisse Rollins attended Nancy's trial every day, sitting together in the front row and holding hands. I thought the sight of them would make Nancy chew off her own tongue. But while she was getting life, Ed and Charisse ran into problems of their own. Ed couldn't lead workouts for ogling women, and doctors didn't want to come to work for a couple of lovebirds. The clinic's clientele wandered away to other miracle workers. I drove down Lomas the other day and noticed a "For Lease" sign in front of the clinic. Somehow, seeing that made up for the times when Mystery Meat sent me airborne.

Boyd Chilton attended the trial, too, but only to keep up appearances. While Nancy awaited trial, he filed for divorce. His girlfriend, whom I'd last seen in bed on her knees, has begun appearing on TV commercials for Chilton Motors, hanging on the arm of her man, both of them wearing big white cowboy hats. The state attorney general has taken up the Gazette's investigation of the crooked car dealers. Felicia says Boyd and the others will be indicted any day now.

Melvin Haywood pieced his life back together after being thoroughly shook up by the police questioning and the accusations against him. He showed up in court the day Nancy was sentenced and was swarmed by news-people as he left. They finally crowded him to a halt on the courthouse steps. The first reporter to stick a microphone in Melvin's face was none other than Jake Steele, who'd ridden Felicia's exposé into a new job at Channel Seven.

Haywood's face hardened when he recognized Steele, and I knew what was coming. The little turtle cracked Steele on the nose with a sweet right uppercut that snapped his head back and sent blood flying. Steele crumpled to the ground.

They played the tape on TV again and again. Haywood wouldn't discuss why he'd done it, and Steele acted like he had no idea. But I knew some rumormonger had told Haywood that a pool boy had serviced more than the swimming pool many years ago. Melvin finally had an outlet for all the jealousy built up within him. It cost him some more time in court, but he seemed satisfied.

I used my VCR to record the footage off the evening news. I've watched it about a hundred times. It looks particularly good in slow motion.

Haywood paid me a fat bonus. I bought myself a new camera.

Dub has officially moved back in with Mama, when they're not on the road together. It's weird that two people can be apart for nearly thirty years and then just pick up again as if nothing ever happened. But love is strange.

As for Felicia and me, we're still crazy in love with each other. She won a bunch of awards for investigative reporting, which made her happy, and she's managing to find a balance between work and home. We're spending more time together, enjoying the extended honeymoon that is our young marriage.

I can't believe, looking back, that I ever doubted her. It's as if I was poisoned by everything I'd seen around The Manor. But I learned my lesson. I'll trust Felicia always. And I'll keep my distance from my neighbors.